Race Against Time

He didn't have to look up to know that the boom above him was bending at the joint, swinging down to meet the lower one. Desperately, he lay the cutters aside and used his fingers to feel for the cable. There it was, right where he'd expected to find it. He fixed the location in his mind, snatched up the cutters, and fished for the cable. Something sharp snagged his hand, tearing skin. The boom pivoted closer, groaning as its massive weight shifted. He squirmed sideways, pressing himself against the hard steel. The cutters closed over something and he clenched his hand. A cable snapped, but the boom kept moving. He had cut the wrong cable.

He lunged again, and felt another cable slip between the blades of the cutters. A thought crossed his mind: **If this isn't the right one, will my body be enough to jam the solar panel?**

The tongue of steel came down against him as his hand grasped convulsively at the handle of the cutters . . . .

STARJACKED!

William Greenleaf

ACE SCIENCE FICTION BOOKS
NEW YORK

**This book is dedicated
to my daughter
Tiffany Ann Greenleaf**

This book is an Ace Science Fiction
original edition, and has never been
previously published.

STARJACKED!

An Ace Science Fiction Book/published by arrangement with
the author

PRINTING HISTORY
Ace Science Fiction edition/April 1987

ISBN: 0-441-78213-2

Ace Science Fiction Books are published by
The Berkley Publishing Group,
200 Madison Avenue, New York, New York 10016.
PRINTED IN THE UNITED STATES OF AMERICA

Chapter 1

"THAT'S her all right," said Leo Blannon.

Erek Speros twisted the vidscreen control to bring the image of the starship in closer. Blannon was right; there was no mistaking the four-circle UNSA logo that stood out dark against the graymetal sheen of the ship's starboard cylinder. Below it, in block-lettered Basic, was a single word: *Copernicus*.

"Let's hook in," Blannon said, his words muffled by the thin cheroot that jutted from the corner of his mouth. He reached above his head to switch on the recording equipment. A set of targeting crosshairs appeared on the forescreen as the recorders began snapping holocells through the *Aire Vega*'s outside visuals. "Still think we're wasting our time?"

Erek didn't respond to Blannon's dig, mainly because he was having a hard time believing what his eyes were telling him. Half the Guard units in this part of Omega Centauri were searching for *Copernicus*. It didn't seem right that he and Blannon had found the ship merely by following a tip from one of Blannon's paid informers.

"C'mon, let's hook," Blannon prompted.

Erek turned to look at him. "We can't do that. We have to get out of here—"

"Don't worry, we will. Right after I get a few shots." Blannon pulled the viewfinder out of its niche under the console and peered through it while he used his free hand to adjust the spectrum filters. "I'm telling you, Erek, this could be the scoop of the decade."

Erek looked back at the screen and felt the anxiety of indecision. It was up to him to decide whether to stay, or to turn tail and run. That was company policy. But in the three years Erek had worked as streamer pilot for Spotlight News, he'd never pulled rank on Blannon, and he was pretty sure that if he did so now, Blannon would find a way to make him wish he hadn't. Besides, he reminded himself, he had already broken company policy by coming out here in the first place.

"Five minutes," he said. "Then we skip."

"Sure," Blannon agreed without taking his eye from the viewfinder. "That's all the time I'll need."

Erek flipped up the keyboard cover and punched in a quick series of commands. Confirmation messages rippled in pale green across the dark face of the readout screen as the stasis system locked the *Aire Vega* into an orbit a hundred kilometers outside that of *Copernicus*. When the system beeped and flashed the all-clear signal, he turned his attention back to the view on the curved forescreen.

From this distance, set against the brilliant backdrop of Omega, *Copernicus* looked more like a child's intricate toy than a full-service sector ship. The ship's main body consisted of two parallel cylinders that were connected hub to hub by slender transportation tubes. The cylinders were locked and stationary when skipping through the stream; but now, in operating mode with an established orbit, they rotated slowly to provide internal gravity. Solar reflector panels, laid in strips along the length of each cylinder, were hinged at the aft side to open at forty-five-degree angles to catch energy from the small yellow star around which *Copernicus* had taken orbit. The panels resembled rigid, gleaming petals.

The *Aire Vega*'s rangefinder display, superimposed at the bottom of the forescreen, reminded Erek of the starship's true size: each cylinder was nearly a kilometer in length and a quarter kilometer in diameter. More than five kilometers separated the two cylinders.

"Why would Cassady bring the ship out here?" he wondered aloud.

Blannon, still working with the recorder's controls, didn't answer. Three weeks ago *Copernicus* had disappeared while on a routine skip to upstream Omega. The skip sequence for the starship and its Guard escort had been cleared in advance, and the escort was several skip zones beyond the point where *Copernicus* broke sequence before the navigation computers relayed that something had gone wrong. By the time the escort vessels returned to the breakout point, *Copernicus* had vanished. Attempts at radio and stream communication met with failure. A sequence backtrack through the navigation computers revealed nothing but confusion. *Copernicus* was lost.

Stream accidents were rare but not unheard of, and it was first assumed that a navigation error had bounced the ship into the oblivion of midstream. But careful digging by NavSec investigators revealed that the ship's disappearance was instead the result of an elaborate plan. Using remote access, somebody had broken the security of the navigation computers on Sierra. A critical program had been changed, sending the ship on a skip sequence that would take it well out of reach of its Guard escort.

Several days later the *Copernicus* crew was found abandoned on an uninhabited Fringe planet. That was when Guard officials learned for the first time that

Xavier Cassady and his men had hijacked *Copernicus*.

A massive search was mounted, but even a full-service sector ship was a very tiny needle in the haystack of Omega Centauri. Nobody had seen a trace of *Copernicus*.

Until now.

Beep, beep, beep.

Startled by the sound, Erek looked down at the commset. The flashing red light indicated an incoming call. Before he could say anything to Blannon, a roar of static burst from the speaker grille, followed immediately by a flat, male voice: "This is *Copernicus*. Please provide identification."

"They have us pegged," Blannon said, leaning back from the viewfinder to look up at the screens. He didn't seem at all alarmed. Or surprised, for that matter. "Give them an ident and see if they'll let us dock."

Erek tore his eyes from the vidscreen to stare at Blannon. *"What?"*

"Didn't think you'd like the idea. But we don't have a choice." Blannon took the cheroot out of his mouth and used it to point to the vidscreen. "Take a look."

Erek leaned forward to peer at the image of *Copernicus*. "What do you mean—?" Then he felt a crawling sensation down his spine. The barrel of a huge power-gun poked out from behind the k-drive web on the starship's port-side hub. Another one was nestled among the mechanical gear around the starboard docking pad, and a third was just coming into view on the curve of the turning cylinder, partly hidden by a solar panel. The powerguns looked horribly out of place—heavy energy weapons were not standard equipment on UNSA sector ships. All three guns had swiveled around to point directly at the *Aire Vega*.

Erek reached for the commset switch.

"Hope you aren't thinking of calling for help," Blannon said. "Cassady may not like it."

Erek hesitated, then drew his hand back. The nearest Guard post was on the planet Semegen IV, three zones downstream. Punching a message through to it wouldn't require a lot of power, but he had no doubt that the communications equipment aboard *Copernicus* would be able to pick it up. He also knew that one of those powerguns would disintegrate a small craft like the *Aire Vega* in a single blast.

"Identification, please," insisted the voice from the commset.

Erek could order the *Aire Vega*'s drive system to skip; once they were inside the k-stream, not even the powerguns would be able to touch them. But that would be as obvious as using the commset. The drive webs, releasing excess energy as they drew power from the engines, would present a heat source to *Copernicus*'s monitors —and a clear sign that the *Aire Vega* was trying to escape.

Which meant that Blannon was right; they didn't have a choice.

Erek drew a steadying breath, then pressed the commset plate and said, "This is *Aire Vega* CHHS-20699 requesting permission to come aboard."

"Permission granted for starboard docking," came the immediate reply. "Technical assistance standing by. Frequency for docking computer transmission is one-zero-two point five. Commence docking procedures now. *Copernicus* out."

The connection was broken before Erek could sign off. He looked over at Blannon.

"Don't worry about it," Blannon said. He jammed the cheroot back into the corner of his mouth and leaned forward to the viewfinder. "If they wanted to use those guns, they could've already."

Small comfort there.

Erek swung the flight control board around, kicked in the stasis engines, and turned the *Aire Vega* toward the hub of *Copernicus*'s starboard cylinder. When they were within a few kilometers of the starship, a blue light came on below the readout screen, indicating a query from *Copernicus*'s docking computer. Erek switched on the *Aire Vega*'s docking lights, then set the transmission frequency and punched the three-key combination that would relinquish stasis control to the docking computer. An airlock door sphinctered open at the cylinder's hub and the *Aire Vega* nosed inside. The vidscreens blurred momentarily, then cleared to an interior view of the docking bay—a cylindrical cavern that extended ten meters or more toward the center of the ship.

Still under the control of the starship's docking computer, the *Aire Vega* hung in the center while the bay rotated around it. Light washed out from concentric luminous strips. A single technician working at a stationary control panel high on a perch against the far wall turned to stare at the *Aire Vega* through the bubble of his helmet. Several other control panels around the chamber's perimeter were activated but unattended.

"Not much business," Blannon observed.

Erek watched the stern-view screen as the outer door narrowed and closed. A few minutes were required for pressure to build, then a row of monitor lights flashed green. He pressed a single key in response. The docking chamber's inner door opened with a muffled mechanical sound, and the *Aire Vega*'s stasis drive fired briefly to move the small craft into the hangar.

"There it is," said Blannon.

Erek looked up at the screens and saw several stub-nosed UNSA shuttlecraft and a few civilian streamers. Then, in the back of the hangar, he saw what Blannon was talking about: a large ship, black, with UNSA markings on its mid-fuselage. The fore and aft drive webs identified it as a streamer, although it also had the streamlined nose and swept-back wings that were required for high-speed atmosphere flight.

Only one kind of ship was designed like that. It was a Guard warship.

"The *Wasp*," Blannon said. He took a drag on the

cheroot and released a cloud of smoke. "Cassady's still got it after all."

Erek's eyes remained fixed on the warship. The *Wasp* was the most powerful fighting machine ever designed. Cassady had already used it once to hijack *Copernicus*. Speculation over the past few weeks had centered on what he was planning for an encore.

Before Erek could pursue that thought, the *Aire Vega* began to swing around to come in line with one of the hangar's landing strips. Correcting movements jostled him gently in his chair. The strips—a dozen or more spaced along the length of the hangar—rotated independent of the cylinder. At the moment, the docking computer held the strip beneath the *Aire Vega* stationary relative to the craft. After the craft's struts engaged it, the strip began moving. Its speed gradually matched that of the cylinder, and Erek felt the first gentle tug of gravity. Lines of data rolled across the readout screen as the *Aire Vega*'s stasis system confirmed with the starship's docking computer that the procedure had been completed successfully. Gravity had reached nearly one-quarter normal—as high as it would get this close to the cylinder's axis.

Erek keyed a series of answers to the docking computer's queries. When the all-clear came, he flipped the sequence of safety locks at the back of the console. Telltales winked green and latches clicked inside the hatch cover behind him.

Blannon had already released his safety harness and swiveled around. When the final latch snapped into place, he pressed the release bar. The hatch cover opened with a pneumatic hiss. Erek put the console on standby and shrugged out of his harness.

As he and Blannon ducked through the hatchway, a door slid open in the hangar wall to their right, and three men stepped through. They took positions to cover the *Aire Vega* with drawn weapons.

Chapter 2

TWO of the men carried full-sized carbines of a design that could punch a hole through half-inch steel on tight focus. One was broad-shouldered and dark, the other lean and blond. Both handled the carbines in a way that showed they knew how to use them.

The third man was clearly the one in charge. He was slight of build, only a little taller than Erek, with dark hair and a narrow face with an oddly straight lower lip. He would have had the look of a dapper businessman or a merchant trader except for the swath of scar tissue that dimpled his left cheek and ran down his neck under the collar of his brown fatigues.

"Step down, please." The thin man spoke Basic, but with an accent Erek couldn't place. One of the Fringe sectors, probably. "Keep your hands where I can see them. Don't make any sudden moves."

Erek risked a glance around the hangar. The *Aire Vega* had come down on the middle landing strip, placing it almost in the exact center of the hangar. Erek could see the openings of several corridors that presumably led to the inner part of the ship, but the nearest was at least twenty meters away. Too far to make a run for. An elevator was closer, but the doors were shut, and there was no way to guess whether or not a carriage waited behind them. Partly hidden by one of the nearby streamers was a guardrail that jutted up from the gray-metal deck; Erek decided it probably adjoined a stairwell that led to a service deck below. If he and Blannon got a chance to make a break—which didn't seem likely —they would have to try for that.

"I won't tell you again," said the man.

"Looks like we've run into a nest of brigs," Blannon said out of the corner of his mouth. "What do you think we should do?"

"Exactly what he tells us," Erek said, keeping his voice low. He was sure Blannon was right. The high-energy carbines were favorites of the bands of marauding Fringe outlaws known as brigs and the brown fatigues had come to be traditional garb for the more successful brig operations.

"Just what I was thinking. Let me do the talking." Blannon grinned, showing a row of strong white teeth, and strode down the ramp with his hand extended. "How do you do, sir. Leo Blannon with Spotlight News." He came to a stop when the other two used their weapons to block his way. The grin remained fixed in place. "That isn't necessary."

The man gave Blannon a hard stare, shifted it to Erek, then back to Blannon. Erek was used to the double take. Blannon was red-faced and forty pounds overweight, with bushy eyebrows and white hair cut so close that from a distance he looked bald. His aggressive manner derived as much from his physical appearance as from the expressive self-confidence that was a natural part of him. By contrast, Erek was slender and slightly below average height, with fair skin, fine brown hair, and hazel eyes that would never win a contest of intimidation. In Blannon's company, Erek tended to be overlooked, which didn't bother him in the least.

"Any others inside?" the man asked.

"No, sir," Blannon answered. "Do you work for Colonel Cassady?"

The man ignored him. "Check it out."

The blond man brushed past Erek and Blannon, took the ramp in three strides, and ducked through the *Aire Vega*'s open hatchway. A moment later he reappeared, nodded to the one in charge, and resumed his position.

"We represent a major news agency," Blannon went on before the other man could speak. "We have a few questions. Am I correct in assuming this is a military operation under the direction of Colonel Cassady?"

The man stared across at Blannon with no perceivable change in expression. Unabashed, Blannon plunged ahead.

"There were forty of Captain M'Hing's stasis technicians on the ship when it was hijacked. Are they still aboard? Why weren't they released with the rest of the crew?"

The man reached out quickly, plucked the cheroot out of Blannon's fingers, dropped it to the metal deck, and crushed it with the heel of his boot. "Cuff them."

The one who had checked inside the *Aire Vega* stepped around to pull Blannon's arms behind him and bind them together with wristcuffs. Another pair of cuffs were clamped over Erek's arms. When the man stepped back around, Erek saw that he held a control pad.

"What are Colonel Cassady's plans now that he has taken possession of the ship?" Blannon asked.

The man with the wristcuff controller made a quick adjustment. Erek's arms tingled. The cuffs were set for close range. If Blannon and Erek stepped outside that range—by trying to escape, for example—the cuffs would send focused electrical charges into their arms. A few of those charges could knock a man out. A few more could kill him.

"Now we can proceed," said the thin man. "My name is Victor Troy." He paused, watching Blannon. "You've heard of me?"

"Sure. You and your brother used to run the biggest brig operation in Omega. Smuggling, mostly. Kept a tight hand on it until the Guard put you out of business." Blannon grinned. "You slipped away and let your brother take the fall. Pretty crafty. Is he still in prison?"

Troy stiffened, and the scar tissue on his cheek went scarlet. Erek cast a sideways glance at Blannon. If he had been probing for a reaction, he couldn't have asked for more.

"How did you find this ship?" Troy asked in a flat voice.

"I'll be glad to discuss that," Blannon said. "But first I want to speak to Colonel Cassady. And I'd like to know what you're planning to do with that warship in the hangar, the *Wasp*—"

Troy must have given a signal to the man with the control pad, because the next thing Erek knew he was writhing on the deck with white-hot bolts of agony shooting up both arms. When it stopped, he couldn't do anything but lie there shaking.

"How did you find this ship?" Troy repeated. His words came from the far end of a long tunnel.

Erek blinked, trying to clear his vision. Above him, Blannon was hunched over, taking deep breaths. His face was strangely pale. Erek struggled to his feet, gritting his teeth as the cuffs bit into his throbbing wrists.

"We've been running a grid search of this sector," Blannon said, his voice subdued. "We knew *Copernicus* had to be in orbit somewhere outside the main traffic lanes, so we stuck to the Fringe. That narrowed it down for us.''

It was weak and Troy knew it. "How many ships are in this grid?"

Blannon hesitated, then said, "Just us . . . "

"With a single ship, the chances of finding us would be a million to one."

Blannon shrugged. "We got lucky."

Troy's eyes flicked to Erek, studying him briefly before returning to Blannon. A sound that may have been a sigh escaped his lips.

"I want answers. We'll get them one way or another. If the cuffs don't do the job, we'll take you upstairs and see what a blackwitch can do."

Erek felt his skin crawl, as much from the cold certainty in Troy's voice as from what he was threatening to do. Erek had never seen a blackwitch, but he knew what it could do. The blackwitch delivered jolts of focused energy directly to the central nervous system. It was illegal, but readily available for the right money. Nobody held out against the 'witch and nobody survived more than a few of its ministrations.

"You can avoid that," Troy went on in his business-like tone, "by telling me the truth right now."

"I've already done that," Blannon said calmly.

Erek could understand why Blannon didn't want to reveal how he'd found *Copernicus*; if Troy didn't know that somebody aboard the ship had sent out a distress call, Blannon didn't want to enlighten him. But Erek couldn't help wondering: *Will he really let them use the 'witch on us?*

Troy nodded at the blond man. Erek braced himself as the man reached for the wristcuff controller.

Crack!

The blond man's head snapped sideways and his eyes widened in surprise. Then his legs buckled and he went down in low-gravity slow motion. Something that looked like a small steel ball bounced and rattled across the deck.

Erek coiled as much strength as he could into his legs and threw himself into the big man who still stood across from him. It was like hitting a block of stone. Half dazed, Erek stepped back and looked up. The man was staring over Erek's head at something farther out in the hangar. When he thumbed the safety and brought the muzzle of the carbine up, Erek kicked him as hard as he could in the groin. The man grunted and took a step backward. Erek heard the thin snap, and felt the hot breath of the carbine uncomfortably close to his ear. He charged again while the man was still off-balance, driving him back with his shoulder in the man's chest. The man stumbled over the flange of the landing strip and went down, banging his head hard against the graymetal deck. He lifted himself up on one elbow, then the whites of his eyes showed and he fell back. Erek felt a twang from the wristcuff as he struggled to keep his balance —not easy with his hands bound behind him.

The snapping sound of a sizzler came from behind him. He turned and saw Troy down on one knee, firing at a steamcraft that was parked high on the deck's curve. The graymetal hull glowed briefly where bolts of energy lanced into it. Leo Blannon had stepped back out of the line of fire.

Then Erek saw movement behind the streamer's landing strut. Something hissed through the air, and Troy's weapon spun out of his hand. He was after it even before it hit the deck, but he stopped when a shrill voice came from beyond the parked streamer:

"Stop right there!"

Troy came to his feet. His face wore no expression, but the scarred tissue of his cheek flamed bright red. Two figures stepped out from behind the parked streamer. They had been concealed partly by the streamer's landing struts and partly by their size.

"Well . . . " For once Blannon was at a loss for words. Erek stared in open amazement as the two figures approached. The girl who had issued the stern order couldn't have been more than nine years old. The boy was older, maybe fourteen or fifteen. In his hand was a black, evil-looking handgun of a kind Erek had never seen before.

"Give me the controller," the girl said in a clear, direct voice. She and the boy stopped a few paces away.

Troy made no move to obey. The blood had drained from his face now to leave it deathly pale. When he spoke, Erek knew he was fighting to control his voice.

"You shouldn't have come out. You won't make it back this time."

If the statement was meant to frighten her, the girl was having none of it. She had delicate features and close-cropped hair, and dark eyes that expressed an alert self-confidence. Her black skin glistened with sweat. She wore an UNSA uniform shirt that hung past her knees. A large pouch was cinched to her waist with a cord. The boy was tall and thin, with ash-blond hair and pale blue eyes. He wore a pair of knee-length shorts that may once have been white.

"Don't push me, Troy," the girl said. "There's nothing I'd like better than to put one of these balls right between your ugly eyes." She gripped her weapon, and for the first time Erek realized it was a primitive hunting sling with a tubular metal frame and heavy elastic cord. That was what she must have used to hit the blond man, and to disarm Troy. Erek's eyes measured the distance back to the streamer up on the curve of the deck. Twenty meters at least, and both her shots had found their targets with pinpoint accuracy.

Troy looked at the sling, then at the two men who lay on the floor. The one Erek had hit was beginning to make groaning sounds; the other was still out cold. Troy reached down, picked up the control pad, and tossed it toward the girl. The boy intercepted it deftly with one hand. He studied it briefly as if he suspected that Troy might somehow have done something harmful to it, then passed it along to the girl. She worked the digital control with agile fingers. Both sets of cuffs beeped and opened.

"Hey, thanks," Blannon said as he shook himself free of the cuffs. "I don't know who you are, but that was a great—"

"Save it," the girl interrupted. She nodded toward Troy. "Put the cuffs on him. And make it quick. We don't have much time."

"Sure." While Erek rubbed the sting out of his arms, Blannon stepped across to snap the cuffs over Troy's thin wrists. Troy stood rigid; he did not try to resist. The girl turned the knob and Erek saw Troy's lips tighten. She turned it farther and he released an involuntary grunt of pain.

Before Erek had time to decide whether the girl was jabbing Troy in order to make a point, or merely to see him squirm, the elevator door at the far side of the hangar hissed open and three men stepped out.

The boy's reaction was lightning fast. He snatched the control pad out of the girl's hand and flung it straight at the elevator. Troy screamed with pain and ran after it with his hands clenched tightly behind his back. More men came out of the elevator and gathered in a confused knot, watching Troy as he raced straight toward them. Erek thought he saw a black and gray UNSA uniform among them.

"Come on!" the girl hissed, already running. Erek reached the guardrail a few steps behind her and found that it was part of a metal stairway that spiraled downward. The girl reached for the handgrip and swung herself easily down through the opening. Erek paused to glance back over his shoulder. Troy lost his footing and went down, and lay squirming on the graymetal deck with his hands still clasped behind him. The ragged group of men was running toward him now, still ten meters away.

"Let's *go!*" The girl was already halfway down the stairs.

Erek went down the steps as fast as he could, with Blannon and the boy close on his heels. By the time they reached the bottom, Troy's cries of pain had been replaced by shouted orders and the sound of boots pounding across the deck.

The stairway led to a narrow, low-ceilinged corridor. The girl turned right and went a short distance to another narrow passage, then turned left and followed the passage to a heavy sealed door. She wrenched the dogs and leaned back on her heels to swing the door open. As they filed through, Erek heard the clatter of boots on the metal stairs behind them, then the door closed with the faint sucking sound of sealing expanders. They were in a vast, open-bayed repair shop.

"Where are we going?" Blannon asked the girl.

She didn't answer, but led them at a long slant across the room to a waiting elevator in the far wall. When they were all inside, she scanned the control panel, then punched three keys in rapid succession. The doors slid shut and the carriage dropped with a suddenness that made Erek grab the safety rail. Only then did the girl turn to look up at Blannon.

"How soon will your backup units get here?"

Blannon gave her a blank stare. "Backup units?"

"You brought some, didn't you?" She looked at him more closely, then shifted her eyes to Erek. "Aren't you undercover agents of the Guard?"

Blannon issued a bark of laughter. "Hardly. I'm a news reporter with Spotlight. Erek's my pilot."

She stared at him through a moment of dead silence. Then:

"Didn't our message get through? Isn't that why you're here?"

"Message?"

"The distress call," Erek interjected. "They must have sent it."

"Oh." Blannon looked slightly uncomfortable. "It got through, but only to us." He didn't explain the rest, which Erek thought was just as well. The girl wouldn't have liked it. A commclerk in a Guard post three zones downstream had snagged a garbled stream transmission that claimed to be from *Copernicus*. Most of the message was lost, but the clerk had gotten enough to realize that the message was a call for help. He had tracked the signal before it faded, then decided to earn some extra script by selling the coordinates to Leo Blannon instead of reporting them to his section chief. Blannon had a reputation for paying well, and for protecting his sources. This wasn't the first time his reputation had paid off in a good tip. Nor was it the first time it had gotten him and Erek in trouble.

The girl turned to look at the boy. He gazed around as if his mind were light-years away. Footsteps hurried past in the corridor outside.

"We'll have to take them back," she said.

The flat expression on the boy's face did not change.

"Take us back where?" Blannon asked.

"To see Gillie."

"Is he one of the stasis technicians?"

That got no answer. Blannon shifted his eyes to the tall boy. Erek knew what he was thinking. A few days after Cassady and his men hijacked *Copernicus*, they shuttled Captain M'Hing and nearly six hundred of the ship's crew members to an uninhabited planet in upstream Omega, along with metalfilm tents, an emergency beacon set on programmed delay, and enough supplies to get them through the few days until the beacon would send out its call for help. Cassady had kept forty technicians aboard, presumably to operate the ship's complex stasis control system.

But there had been no mention of children. As far

as Erek knew, the crew and passenger lists had been checked and double-checked. Only the stasis techs were missing.

Before Blannon could ask another question, the elevator slowed and came to a stop. The girl turned her attention to the control board.

"Where are we?" Blannon asked.

"Tenth level. We'll have to switch to another elevator."

"How come?"

"Troy's men will get a fix on us if we stay with the same one too long."

The doors whispered open. Two men stood in the corridor outside. They turned toward the elevator, surprise registering on their faces an instant before they grabbed for their sidearms.

Chapter 3

THE girl's sling thrummed; a steel ball slapped into flesh. One of the men yelped, grabbed his wrist, and staggered back as his weapon hit the carpeted floor. The other one brought his sizzler up and found himself staring at the muzzle of the boy's gun.

It had all happened in an instant, but now time seemed to stop as everyone waited through a tense silence. The man with the sizzler wore UNSA grays—a sergeant, by the stripes on his shoulder tab. He stood with his arm outstretched and rigid. A muscle worked along his jaw. The other man wore sweat-stained fatigues. He was older, craggy-looking, with a patch of synthetic flesh where his left eye should have been. He hunched against the corridor wall across from the elevator, still holding his wrist. His face was a mixture of rage and pain.

"Shoot them," he snarled. "You heard what Troy said. They don't have to be alive when we bring 'em back."

"Don't be stupid!" the girl snapped back. She crouched just inside the elevator door. Her sling, armed with a new ball, was gripped tightly in both hands. "That gun has a hair trigger. Even if you shoot first, it'll still kill you."

The boy stood like stone, the gleaming skin of his face stretched tautly over the bones. Sweat sheened his upper body. His eyes did not move from the man with the sizzler. His finger twitched on the trigger of the big gun.

"C'mon," prompted the man with the patch. "It's a bluff. Shoot them!"

Sweat beaded on the young sergeant's face. His eyes were still on the muzzle of the boy's gun. Then all the strength went out of his arm and the sizzler fell to his side. He glanced sideways at the other man. "I don't take orders from Victor Troy. And I don't shoot kids."

Erek released pent-up breath. The man with the patch snorted with disgust.

"Set the safety and toss it over here," the girl said.

The man did as she ordered; the sizzler bounced once on the elevator floor and landed at Erek's feet. He started to reach for it, then saw the boy's eyes on him and changed his mind.

"Now that one." The girl motioned to the weapon the other man had dropped. "Don't pick it up. Slide it across with your foot."

"That's mine!" the man flared, pushing himself away from the wall. "Don't be givin' it to no kids!"

"Shut up!" the girl snapped. She lifted her sling and stretched the cord tighter. "Stay where you are."

The man glared at her with his single eye, but he didn't come any closer. The other one used the toe of his boot to nudge the gun across the floor and into the elevator. It was a pellet gun—the lethal kind that sprayed a hundred rounds a second. At close range, it was more dangerous than an energy weapon. Erek wondered if it were mere coincidence that the girl had gone after it first.

The boy picked up both weapons and jammed them into the frayed waistband of his pants.

"You'll pay for that," snarled the man with the eye patch.

"Sure," the girl said derisively. "Get back against the wall."

After the two men had moved away from the elevator, she jabbed at the control panel. The doors closed and the elevator shot down, then jerked to a stop at the next level. At the girl's direction, they left the carriage and turned right to move quickly down a wide, carpeted hallway to another elevator.

"That was close," Blannon puffed when they were in the carriage and underway once more. "Think we'll run into more of them?"

"No reason they should've been on the tenth level," the girl muttered.

"Yeah, but do you think—"

"How'm I s'posed to know?" she snapped.

"That man wearing black and gray is obviously one of Cassady's men," Blannon went on, unfazed. "I might've seen another guardsman up there in the hangar. Any idea why they're working with brigs?"

"No." She punched a button and the elevator came to a stop. "We'll switch again here."

Moving in a direction that was subjectively "down," they worked their way outward through the concentric levels of the massive cylinder. Blannon maintained a thoughtful silence.

When the door slid open for the last time, a blast of hot, humid air rushed into the elevator. They had reached ground level. Outside, a concrete platform was awash with bright sunlight.

When Blannon took a step toward the door, the girl stopped him.

"We'll wait here."

He turned to look down at her in surprise. "Why?"

"Because I said so."

"Any particular reason?"

"It'll be dark in a few minutes. That'll give us better cover."

Blannon looked doubtfully out through the open door. "I don't think it's too likely that—"

"What you think don't matter." She turned on him, her black eyes flashing. "Troy'd be pulling out your fingernails by now if we hadn't got you away from him. You've already been more trouble than you're worth. Now shut up and let me do the thinking. I'm better at it."

Erek had never seen Leo Blannon cowed by anyone's anger. But now he grinned sheepishly and fell silent. The boy stood motionless in the corner.

They waited. Erek looked out through the open door. Stretching away from the concrete platform was a broad grassy area, its center dominated by a multitiered fountain. At the far edge of the grass stood a grove of shade trees. Behind that lay a large pond and a dock with a few paddleboats floating around it. Erek had been inside several sector ships, and he knew that a recreational area would normally be crowded with off-duty crew members. This one was deserted, and the only sound breaking the silence was the faint splash of the fountain.

Erek lifted his eyes to the hub structure at the far end of the cylinder—a mirror image of the structure they had just come through. The interior of this cylinder had the same basic design as that of other sector ships. There were no individual buildings. Instead, at each hub was a single massive structure that was comprised of hundreds of offices, staterooms, dining lounges, theaters, and other functional units. Each hub structure jutted nearly a third of the way into the cylinder at the floor, angling back toward the outer wall at the center of the hub in order to catch maximum light and heat from the window strips. The inner third of the cylinder's floor was used primarily for recreation.

"Sure is hot," Blannon commented. "Solar panels

must not be working right.''

Erek glanced up through the open door at the window strip high above them and blinked against the brilliant glare. Temperatures in habitable areas of sector ships were controlled mainly by the solar reflector panels. The panels focused warmth and sunlight through the window strips onto the land areas below. The strips, six in each cylinder, stretched across the longitudinal axis, alternating with the land regions around the circumference of the cylinder. The solar panels were adjustable; as they moved, the angle at which sunlight struck the land regions changed, allowing control over the length of day and the intensity of incoming light.

''Get ready,'' the girl said abruptly, interrupting Erek's thoughts. Then he realized that the light around them was fading; above the platform, the brilliant glare shifted as the panels moved. By the time they had stopped, the concrete platform outside the elevator was left in a dusky glow.

''Let's go.''

They stepped out of the elevator and the girl led them to a metal plate that was set into the concrete near the edge of the platform. There was no servo control; she grasped the slot at one end and struggled with the plate until Erek offered a hand. She gave him a sour look, but moved to make room for him. The plate folded open to reveal a metal ladder that continued downward into the darkness. The girl pulled up the handgrip extension, locking it into place. Then she opened her pouch and took out a portable lantern.

''You first,'' she said, prodding Blannon with the lantern.

Blannon glanced uneasily at the dark hole, then grasped the ladder and gingerly climbed down. Erek followed, then the girl. The boy came last, pulling the extension and its cover back into place, leaving them in total darkness until the girl snapped on her lantern. In the backwash of light, Erek could see that they stood

in a narrow, low-ceilinged passageway that stretched
straight along into darkness ahead of them. It was a little cooler here than topside, and the air had a faintly
musty odor. The girl reduced the beam to a dim glow,
then turned without a word and started down the
passageway.

"Where are we going?" Blannon asked, falling into
step beside her. His words echoed eerily from the graymetal walls.

"To see Gillie," replied the girl.

"You still haven't told us who he is."

"He's my brother."

They emerged into a wider corridor and turned left.
The ceiling was still uncomfortably close, laced with air
ducts and electrical conduits. Massive support pylons
were spaced at regular intervals along the walls. Beyond
the dim pool of light was utter blackness.

Blannon asked: "How come there aren't any lights
down here?"

"Gillie rigged up a control so we can turn them off,"
the girl said. "Keeps the brigs away. They get lost in the
dark."

"Smart move." Blannon was beginning to breathe
hard with the fast pace. "Gillie must have a good head
on his shoulders."

"He does."

They turned into an intersecting passage, went past a
control station where a bank of microprocessors sent information out through clicking relays. Hundreds of tiny
monitor lights winked at them in the darkness.

"You and Troy know each other?" Blannon asked.

"We've tangled a few times," the girl admitted.

"You have an exceptional talent with that sling.
Where'd you learn to use it like that?"

The girl stopped abruptly and turned to glare up at
him. "You always talk this much?"

"Well . . . " He blinked against the beam of light that

was fixed directly in his face.

"Keep it zipped. If we run into a repair crew, it would be nice to get past them without them seeing us." She turned around and started down the corridor. "Not much chance if you keep flapping your jaw."

Blannon usually didn't take well to personal reprimand. But he knew how to keep his priorities straight, and Erek was grateful that he remained silent as they followed the girl's faint beam of light. One thing they didn't need right now was a confrontation of egos.

They were in the part of the starship known as the basement, between the cylinder's inner developed surface and the outer hull. Erek could understand why Troy's men would have difficulty finding their way around down here. The basement was a maze of corridors and tubeways—miles of them, and the only directional help Erek could see were the wall placards at each intersection. The placards might have offered guidance to a technician familiar with their jargon, but they meant nothing to him. He suspected they would be as meaningless to the brigs.

After they had walked a long distance, the girl stopped suddenly and held up a hand for silence. Then she used the handle of her sling to rap three times on the graymetal wall. An answering series of taps sounded almost immediately, and a swath of pale light appeared on the floor a dozen meters ahead of them.

"Come on," she said.

When they got closer, Erek saw that the light came from a storage alcove adjoining the corridor. Metalfilm crates had been stacked to form a wall between the corridor and the alcove, with only a small opening at one end to serve as a door. Stenciled on the side of each crate was a seven-digit number, along with the words PROPERTY OF UNITED NATIONS SPACE ADMINISTRATION—DEEP SPACE UNIT 12A. Some of the crates had been opened. Boxes of food rations were stacked in one corner of the alcove, and piles of blankets that might have served as sleeping mats were folded neatly in another.

Waiting at the makeshift door was a tall, thin boy. He looked at the men curiously as they approached.

"They ain't with the Guard," the girl said as she lowered her pouch to the floor. "They blundered into Troy. We had to get 'em out."   .

"You're not guardsmen?" The boy's eyes moved back and forth between Erek and Blannon. "Who are you?"

"I'm a reporter," Blannon said. "Erek's my pilot."

"A reporter?"

It took a while to get the explanations sorted out. After that came an awkward round of introductions. The thin boy was Gillie. The black girl's name was Joby, and the silent one, who had gone to stand with his back against the far wall, was Richard.

Blannon's eyes flicked to the pale-skinned Gillie, and back to Joby. "You said Gillie is your brother?"

"Yes," Joby said and busied herself with her pouch. "So's Richard."

Blannon studied her with a quizzical expression. Then he shook his head slightly and turned back to Gillie. "Looks like you've set up housekeeping." He eased his weight down onto one of the crates and cast a glance around the alcove. "Joby said you sent out a call to the Guard. Is there a commset down there?"

"Sort of." Gillie nodded his head toward a dim corner of the alcove. Erek turned and could barely distinguish the outline of an oddly shaped assortment of objects resting atop a pair of crates. "We found some spare parts in a storage room on the fourth level and patched together a set. But we don't have a serial interface for the readout screen. So far, we've only been able to get one call through. We thought we'd reached the Guard, but . . . " He shrugged. "Guess we'll have to try again."

"What's a serial interface?"

"Fancy name for a cable that connects the commset processor to the readout screen. We've been able to use the 'set to monitor CommSec communications from the ship. That's how we knew you were docking. But without the screen, punching a message any distance through the stream is tough. There's no way to keep track of frequency and stream coordinates."

Erek understood the problem. The intricacies of stream communication called for a perfect balance between transmission frequency and stream coordination factors. Transmission frequencies could be set, but stream coordination factors came in random patterns; you had to track the factors and then set the frequencies to match. Keeping that balance without the benefit of viewing the factors on a readout screen would be all but impossible.

"Why couldn't you get the cable?" he asked.

"It's usually connected to the screen housing," the boy answered. "But the only screen we could find had already been cannibalized. We've looked all over for another one."

"Where's the flight deck?"

"Fifth level. We thought about trying to get up there, decided it was too risky."

"Is there a CommSec office around here?" Erek asked. There had to be some way to get another message out.

"Seventh level," Gillie replied. "We were going to check that out if the commset didn't work."

The discussion lapsed into silence. Blannon broke it, looking thoughtfully at Gillie. "You're—what, maybe thirteen years old?"

"Fourteen," the boy corrected. "Standard Terran years."

Blannon grinned. "Fourteen, then. Where'd you learn how to build a commset?"

Erek had been wondering the same thing. Even a

trained CommSec technician would have had difficulty assembling an interstream commset from spare parts.

"My uncle was—" Gillie began, but was stopped by Joby.

"They don't need to know about that!"

The boy's eyes slid away from Blannon. "Well . . ."

Blannon laughed and reached across to give the boy a good-natured slap on the shoulder. "That's not important. What is important is what's happening on this ship. Have you heard anything with that commset of yours that could give us a clue about Cassady's plans?"

Gillie shook his head. "Most ship's communications go through the intercom system. That's hard-wired. We don't have any way of listening in."

"Do you know why Troy and his band of brigs are involved? Strange bedfellows for a man like Xavier Cassady."

"I've been wondering about that, too," Gillie said.

"Hmmm."

Another lengthy pause was broken by Gillie. "How long will it take the Guard to find us?"

"No way to tell," Blannon answered. "They're putting a lot of manpower into the search, but Omega's a big place. Might take a while unless they get better information to go on."

"Great," Joby said. She got up and headed toward the rear of the alcove.

Blannon folded one leg over the other and went through the process of lighting a cheroot. Puffing smoke, he peered up at Gillie and Erek.

"The way I see it, we have two choices. We can sit around and wait for Cassady and Troy to make their next move, or we can work out a plan to find out what they're up to and get the information out to the Guard." He offered his toothy grin. "Personally, I never was one for waiting for things to happen."

Chapter 4

"HOW much farther?" Blannon wheezed.

"We'll be there in a few minutes," Gillie replied. "Then we can head upstairs."

After a few more paces Blannon spoke again: "Think it'll be cooler up there?"

The boy's only response was a slight chuckle. They had been following the narrow beam from Gillie's lantern for the past half hour, cautiously making their way through the broad aisles that crisscrossed the starboard cylinder's cargo hold. Metalfilm crates were stacked to the ceiling on each side of them, interspersed with drums of chemicals and fuels, cases of foodstuffs, and uncrated machinery ranging from plastiform sprayers to massive earthmoving equipment. Everything was lashed to dividing bulkheads or hold-down posts.

Gillie seemed to know the way well enough, and barely glanced at the cryptic directional placards that were spaced at regular intervals. Blannon walked beside him;

Erek and Joby followed close behind, with Richard lagging by several paces.

Erek hoped that Gillie was as sure of his way as he seemed to be; his stomach tightened at the thought of getting lost down here with no other light but the feeble beam provided by the boy's lantern.

"You sure the brigs don't come down this way?" Blannon asked.

"I've never seen any in the cargo hold," Gillie answered. "All this stuff is used for planetary development. There's nothing here they would want."

"Don't worry," Joby piped in. "We won't let mean old Troy get his hands on you."

That got a chuckle out of Blannon, although it was a little strained. Erek wondered if Blannon were having the same second thoughts he was having. They'd all agreed that they had to find another interstream commset if they hoped to get a message through to the Guard post on Semegen IV. It was Blannon who suggested they go up to the seventh-level CommSec office. Erek had been against the idea from the start—in his opinion, getting a call out to the Guard wasn't worth the risk of falling into Troy's hands again.

But popular opinion ran against him. According to Gillie, there were only thirty or forty brigs on the ship, and even fewer guardsmen. He thought they had a good chance of reaching the CommSec office without running into any of them. So they struck a compromise. A scouting mission. If they could reach the CommSec office and get out a message to Semegen IV, all the better. But if it became obvious that it was too dangerous, they would turn back and try using Gillie's commset without the serial interface.

"Can we rest a minute?" Blannon asked, wheezing.

Gillie turned to look at him. "Sure." He seemed surprised that an overweight middle-aged man couldn't match his pace. "Guess this is as good a place as any."

Joby muttered something about wasting time, but

didn't make an issue of it. She moved ahead to take a position where she had a long view down the corridor. Richard dropped back in the opposite direction.

Blannon looked thoughtfully at him, then turned to Gillie.

"The boy sure isn't a talker."

Gillie hunkered down with his back to the wall. "Richard's a deaf-mute."

"Oh." Blannon frowned. He lowered himself to the floor across from Gillie, stretching his legs out in front of him. Gillie placed the lantern between them so it produced a dim circle of light. Erek leaned back against a large crate, feeling drained by the heat.

"I've been wondering about this guy Cassady," Gillie said. "What do you know about him?"

Blannon answered: "Up until two months ago, he was a full colonel in the Guard. Then he went into business for himself."

"What do you mean?"

"He deserted the Guard while his unit was on field exercises. Took a dozen of his men with him."

Gillie nodded. "I thought it must be something like that. We've seen a few of them, still in uniform. But I couldn't figure out why guardsmen would hijack a sector ship."

"They aren't guardsmen now," Blannon corrected. "They're fugitives. But it's a puzzle all right. Cassady had a spotless record. Commendations, quick promotions. The men who went with him had good records, too. Most were career veterans." He used the back of his sleeve to wipe sweat off his brow. "Somehow, Cassady talked them into leaving all that. Most of them were his cronies from way back. He spent the last several months getting them assigned to the *Wasp*."

"The *Wasp*?"

"Cassady's patrol craft. Class A."

Gillie's eyes widened. "One of those big warships?"

"Afraid so. He took it with him when he deserted."

Blannon hooked a thumb toward the floor. "It's down there in the hangar, along with enough heavy weapons to pulverize a big city in a matter of minutes. Not to mention the stream-jumping warheads. The Guard's a little sore at Cassady for taking those."

That was an understatement. Interstream missiles, capable of delivering a nuclear punch to a target from several skipzones away, were the Guard's deadliest weapons. Erek knew that the loss of the dozen or so missiles carried by the *Wasp* had caused more consternation than the loss of the warship itself.

"That's how he was able to take *Copernicus*," Gillie said. "He had that warship."

Blannon nodded. "Plus some fancy navigation programming to put *Copernicus* right where he wanted it."

That had come out after Captain M'Hing and his crew were rescued from the undeveloped planet in upstream Omega. When the starship broke skip sequence and set out on a new tangent, it was still under control of the NavSec computers on Sierra—and the altered program. The ship popped out of the stream near a white dwarf mass-plus in an uncharted area of Omega, and Captain M'Hing and his crew found themselves facing a fully armed Class A warship—and Xavier Cassady demanding surrender.

Some people blamed Captain M'Hing for what happened to *Copernicus*, but from what Erek could see, the captain had no choice. A single hit with one of those powerguns would have destroyed *Copernicus* and killed everyone aboard.

"I never would've believed Cassady and his men would team up with a bunch of brigs," Blannon said. "He spent most of his career with the Guard cleaning out brig nests."

"They must have something big in mind," Gillie observed.

"Guess so. But Victor Troy isn't even a big-time brig leader any more, not since the Guard put him and his brother out of business. Troy slipped out of the noose, but his organization was yanked out from under him. The Guard's been looking for him ever—"

"Shhh!"

They all turned to stare at Joby. She held up a hand for silence. Then Erek heard it—a distant sound rising above the hum of the basement ventilator fans. Voices echoed off the metal walls. After a moment they faded away.

Gillie scrambled to his feet.

"Sounds carry a long way down here," he said softly. "They probably aren't too close, but we'd better get moving just in case."

Keeping the light dim, they continued down the aisle. Erek could feel the heavy beating of his heart, and he remembered Troy's threat: *If the cuffs don't do the job, we'll take you upstairs and use a blackwitch on you.*

A short distance farther, Gillie turned down a long, narrow passage that led between the plates of one of the cylinder's window strips. They passed several huge outcroppings of machinery that Erek knew must be part of the mechanism that controlled the solar reflector panels outside the ship, then emerged into another passage that led to a metal stairway. They had not heard the voices again, which made Erek feel a little better. Gillie glanced at the wall placard, then took the stairs two at a time. He waited for the others in the soft pool of light at the landing, then grasped the metal handle and pulled the door open just far enough to peer through. Joby pressed close behind him.

"See anyone?" she hissed.

Gillie shook his head, opened the door farther, and slipped through. The others followed as quietly as possible and found themselves in a small maintenance shop with floor-mounted workbenches and repair bays. The lights were low and a fine coating of dust gave the room a general look of disuse. Gillie headed straight across to a door at the far wall. It opened into another stairwell.

"This goes all the way to the seventh level," Gillie said. "We'll come out close to the CommSec office."

"Wouldn't it be easier to take an elevator?" Blannon asked.

Already halfway up the first flight of stairs, Gillie stopped and turned. "Sure. But the brigs are more likely to be using the elevators. The stairs would be safer."

Blannon heaved a sigh and started climbing.

They had to stop twice to let Blannon catch his breath, but eventually they came to a door with a marker identifying the seventh level. Gillie opened it a few inches and looked through. He turned briefly to the others with a finger to his lips. Erek was surprised to see a sizzler in his other hand. All of them were armed; even Erek carried the pellet gun Joby had taken from the man with the eye patch. It had felt awkward and uncomfortable in his hand, so he'd tucked it into the waistband of his slacks.

When Gillie signaled, they all filed through the door and into another wide corridor. They stood for a moment with their backs against the wall, hardly breathing. The hallway was dimly lighted; numbered stateroom doors lined both sides. The only sound was the hum of a distant motor.

Apparently satisfied with the silence, Gillie started to move slowly down the corridor. They went through a small reception area to another passageway that branched off both right and left. Gillie stepped quickly across to another door. This one opened onto a wide lobby furnished with armchairs and low tables. Erek realized what it was even before he saw the double-helix medicenter sign above the reception desk. Beyond the desk stood a set of double doors that were folded open to reveal a wide corridor that stretched straight out away from them. Now Erek could hear sounds suggesting human activity: the whir of a data encoder, the click of computer relays, the muffled buzz-blip of an ECS monitor.

"We'll go past some offices," Gillie said softly. "Then an auditorium. Just beyond that, we'll turn left toward the stasis control section. The CommSec office is just around the corner from that."

Hugging the wall, they moved silently past a dining lounge, men's and women's washrooms, and several administrative offices. Erek risked a glance through each open doorway as he passed. The offices were empty, although some of them had clearly been in recent use.

They passed the auditorium Gillie had mentioned and Erek could see the intersecting corridor not far ahead. The CommSec office should be just around the corner.

Then he heard voices. Gillie came to an abrupt stop, waving frantically for the others to move back against the wall. Several men in brown fatigues walked past the intersection and down the adjoining corridor. Erek's heart hammered inside his chest. If one of them had glanced in their direction . . .

Gillie eased forward to the corner. He peered around after the men, then cautiously looked the other way. He turned back and crooked a finger. By the time Erek reached the intersection, Gillie and Blannon were already around the corner. The brigs were out of sight.

Erek saw that one of the doors down the corridor was identified with a silver plate: UNSA COMMUNICATIONS SECTION—AUTHORIZED PERSONNEL ONLY.

Keeping his back to the wall, Erek moved toward the office. Then he froze. The sounds of conversation drifted through the open doorway. He heard keyboards clacking, computer printers whirring. With a sinking feeling, he realized someone was using the CommSec office.

Then a hand plucked at his sleeve. He whirled around. The door behind him was open to a darkened room. Gillie pulled him inside.

Chapter 5

THE office Xavier Cassady had taken for himself was a small, neat cubicle two levels below the flight deck. The furnishings were simple: woodtone desk with built-in console and dual screens, one swivel chair. Two utilitarian armchairs flanked the desk, and behind it a low credenza held a jo dispenser, a brown mug, and a tidy stack of papers. On the wall above the credenza was a Terran landscape holo that had belonged to the office's former occupant, one of Captain M'Hing's junior navigation officers.

Lieutenant Kurt Hollins waited nervously in one of the straight-backed chairs. He knew why the colonel had chosen this office instead of Captain M'Hing's luxurious suite, or any of the dozen other executive offices that had real wooden furniture and thick carpeting. To Cassady, such amenities were only distractions. This simple room met his needs: Every significant operational event, whether reported by stasis techs or by ship's monitors, was downlinked through descending levels of computer systems to the microprocessor that was part of the desk console.

Cassady had been studying one of those reports for the past several minutes, using console controls to move rapidly from frame to frame while Hollins tried his best to follow on the second readout screen that faced his side of the desk. Victor Troy sat stiffly in the chair beside him.

The tension Hollins felt didn't come from Colonel Cassady. Even though Cassady was revered by the men under his command, he was more friend than superior officer to Hollins. The tension didn't even come from Victor Troy. Rather, the room itself seemed to emanate a wary caution, as if the conflicting personalities of Xavier Cassady and Victor Troy rubbed, creating a friction in the air.

"We have a red-line temperature imbalance at axis G-17," Cassady said abruptly. He punched a series of buttons and the top of his desk cleared to transparency, revealing a three-dimensional schematic of a section of the starboard cylinder near the dockside hub. Cassady used a tracker ball to rotate the view and zoomed in on the glow representing abnormal temperature variations. "Do you have more information on that?"

Hollins answered: "Yes, sir. File eight, volume double-K. There's a problem in one of the solar panel servos."

"Mechanical or ECS control?" Cassady was already punching keys.

"Mechanical. A relief valve in one of the external hydraulic systems failed." Hollins had been Cassady's technical aide for the past six years. Except for a few of the stasis technicians, he was the only man aboard the ship who knew the Environmental Control System. "The secondary has been out for three wakes, but we haven't had a chance to fix it, so the system shut down."

Cassady accepted this with a murmur and a nod. Information was beginning to flow across the readout screen. From the corner of his eye, Hollins saw Troy's hands grip the arms of his chair. He wondered how long Cassady would keep him waiting. He was sure Troy knew why he had been summoned to this office.

"Looks like a major repair job," Cassady observed.

"Yes, sir. I have people working on it. Half a dozen stasis techs and a few bri—" He cleared his throat with a sideways glance at Troy. "A few of Mr. Troy's men. We'll have it repaired by next wake. There's a general report on environmental control in file two, volume M. Current to half an hour ago."

Cassady reached forward to punch in the database keys. He skimmed over a few screens, stopping to examine one more closely. Then he shifted his gaze to Hollins.

"Will ECS last another eight hours?"

Hollins hesitated. He felt Troy's eyes on him. "I think so, sir, barring unforeseen problems. Temperatures are rising throughout the ship. So far they're controllable."

"Are the stasis techs still cooperating?"

"Yes, sir."

"Good." Cassady switched off the desk viewer and leaned back in his chair. His gaze turned slowly to Troy. There was a long silence before Cassady spoke.

"I understand a civilian ship docked a few hours ago."

Now we're into it, Hollins thought. He felt a measure of relief mixed with the heightened tension.

"A news reporter and his pilot," Troy said. "Somehow they found us—"

"Why wasn't I notified?"

The scar across Troy's cheek flamed red. "My men are not under your command, Colonel Cassady." The word colonel was given a slight, derisive emphasis. "You have your own people. I assumed they would report the matter to you."

"They did. But you conducted the interrogation."
The hint of a smile crossed Cassady's face. "Until you
were interrupted by the two kids from the basement,
that is."

Hollins kept his expression carefully neutral. Was
Cassady purposely trying to provoke Troy?

"Do you know how they found the ship?" Cassady
asked.

"Not yet. I've got a search party in the basement—"

"Call them back. The skip window will open in eight
hours. That means we'll reach target in less than ten
hours."

"I know that . . . "

"Will your men be ready?"

"Of course," Troy said. "My men have been ready
for the past three weeks."

Troy's statement brought the tension to a crackling
pitch. The unspoken truth lay between them like an
open wound. There were thirty-five brigs aboard the
ship and only fourteen guardsmen. At this point, each
group needed the other. But after the skip it would be a
different story.

"Call your men back," Cassady said again. "We
can't waste time looking for a news reporter and a
bunch of kids."

"If the Guard knows—"

"If the Guard knew where to find us, they would be
here by now. Have your men report to the flight deck.
There aren't enough people to go around up there as it
is. Getting a ship like this ready for a skip takes time.
And cooperation. We can't afford to miss that window."

Troy sat perfectly still for a long moment. Then:

"Very well." He pushed back his chair and stood,
turned quickly, and left the room.

After the door closed, Cassady leaned back and
rubbed his eyes. Then he swiveled around to the credenza to pull himself a cup of hot jo. As he swung back,

he said, "Can we be ready for that window?"

Hollins had been expecting the question. "Yes, sir, from a technical standpoint. Drive system programming is underway, and the stasis link shouldn't be too much trouble. We've finished the powergun instrumentation. Secondary drivers are in place, and final tests on the weapons systems have already started. The earlier problems in attitude and reaction control have been traced to faulty sensors."

"Good. Will we be able to keep these temperature variations under control?"

"Yes, sir. We're increasing the temperature gradually, as you ordered. We'll have no problem bringing it back down when we need to."

"No sign that Troy suspects what we're doing?"

"None that I've seen."

Cassady nodded. "You've organized a team to take care of the stasis techs, I assume?"

"Yes, sir. Captain Asusa and three others. They'll be ready to enter the flight deck immediately after the skip."

"Good. Is there anything else we need to discuss?"

"No, sir." Hollins rose to his feet and gave a quick salute, then turned and walked toward the door.

"Lieutenant Hollins?"

Hollins turned. "Sir?"

"Don't you think it's about time we dropped the 'sir'?"

Hollins considered the question seriously. "Yes, sir. Maybe so." He turned and left the room.

Cassady remained at his desk, staring at the blank wall for a long time after Hollins had gone. Then he reached into one of the desk drawers and pulled out a small square holocell print: a young woman with long brown hair standing on a grassy lawn with one arm around a small, dark-haired boy. The woman smiled openly at the 'corder; the boy tilted his head and offered a self-conscious grin. He'd been six at the time. In the background was a two-story house of white plastiform. The front porch was surrounded by beds of jewel-tips and yellow sandanna the woman had planted in early spring.

Cassady sagged back against the chair and felt a deep weariness come over him. He drifted back into the past, and a finger of doubt traced its way up his spine—

Then he forced himself to straighten. His eyes remained on the print, but now he used it to give him strength, to renew his sense of conviction. After staring at it for a long moment, he opened the drawer and carefully replaced it in the desk. He glanced at his wristwatch.

Eight hours.

Chapter 6

AFTER they were all crowded into the room with the door closed behind them, Joby had an immediate suggestion:

"Let's jump 'em. There's only two or three in there."

"They might be armed," Gillie cautioned. "It's too risky. Especially if they're brigs."

"We'll surprise 'em. They won't have a chance to get their guns."

Blannon broke in: "Gillie's right. There may only be two or three of them, but if we cause a commotion we'll probably attract a lot more." He grinned and reached out to ruffle Joby's hair, but missed when she scowled and moved away. "Like you said, we sure don't want Troy to get his claws on us again."

The faint sound of footfalls came from the corridor outside. Everyone kept silent until they passed the door and faded away.

Erek saw that the tiny room they had ducked into was a storage cubby. Boxes of writing paper, datachips, and other office supplies were arranged on narrow shelves along the walls. Larger boxes were stacked on the floor. Except for two opened boxes, everything was strapped down as it must have been during the last skip. The single overhead tube cast an uncomfortably bright glare.

"That doesn't mean I'm ready to give up," Blannon went on. He looked around for something to sit on, gave up, and leaned back against a shelf unit. He fished a cheroot out of a front pocket and stuck it in his mouth without lighting it. His eyes went to Erek. "Maybe we could find another commset while we're up here."

"We could look around," Erek said without enthusiasm. He was more interested in getting back to the relative safety of the basement. "That'd be risky, too. Far as I know, the only other place with interstream commsets is the flight deck."

"Hmmm."

A short silence intervened.

"Maybe we can still do something up here."

That was from Gillie. Erek looked up and caught the boy's eyes on him. Gillie offered a self-conscious grin and looked away. But a moment later his eyes came back.

"I was just thinking . . . " he began. He let the words trail off.

Blannon's head swung around. The cheroot dangled from a corner of his mouth. "You were thinking what?"

"Well . . . " Gillie looked at Joby. "It would only take a few seconds to pull a cable out of one of the commsets in that office. If we had a cable, we could take it back to the basement and hook it up to our 'set. We could call the Guard from there."

"Would one of those cables fit your commset?" Blannon asked doubtfully.

"Sure. Serial cables are all the same."

Erek pointed out the obvious flaw in Gillie's idea: "In

order to get the cable, we'd still have to get into the CommSec office."

"Well, yeah," Gillie admitted. "I gave that some thought, too. I'll bet a stasis tech could get in there without much trouble."

Blannon frowned. "I don't follow."

"If the men in there are brigs," Gillie explained, "they probably don't know much about ship's procedures. A stasis tech could make up a convincing story—tell them he needed to borrow an interface cable for another 'set that had broken down. Something like that."

Up until now, Erek had given Gillie credit for having a good head on his shoulders. But the boy was grasping at straws so far out of reach they were nonexistent. "Where would we find a stasis tech? You already said you haven't seen any around here. They're probably all at the flight deck. That's way over at the other end of the cylinder."

"I know." Gillie's eyes moved back to Joby. "We got that shirt out of one of the storage crates in the basement. Isn't it the same kind the stasis techs wear?"

Bemused, Erek turned to look at the tunic that hung past Joby's knees. He hadn't paid much attention to it before, but now he saw that Gillie was right. The diagonal crosshatch in black and gray was the pattern UNSA reserved for its sector ship stasis control technicians.

"I still don't see where this is leading," he said. "Joby could hardly pass as a stasis tech."

Gillie turned his gaze to Erek. "I know *she* couldn't."

Erek stopped outside the open door and drew a deep, steadying breath. From the CommSec office he could hear the irregular clatter of console keys, the whisper of a data encoder, occasional male voices. Other sounds of activity drifted from doorways down the corridor on either side. The storage cubby, with Blannon and the others waiting inside, was directly behind him.

You heard what Troy said. They don't have to be alive when we bring them back.

The words came back from the man with the eye patch. They didn't make Erek feel any better. There in the storage cubby, Erek had come up with a dozen reasons why Gillie's idea wouldn't work. Gillie and Blannon had spent ten minutes telling them why it could.

"The shirt's too big," he said, starting with what he thought was most obvious. "It'll hang on me. Anybody will be able to see it isn't mine."

Joby settled that one. She made them all turn their backs while she exchanged the gray and black tunic for Erek's brown pullover. When Erek pulled on the tunic, it was a perfect fit. His dark slacks weren't UNSA regulation, but they would pass a casual glance.

He tried again: "I don't know anything about stasis control in sector ships. What if somebody asks me a technical question?"

"Based on what Gillie says, you aren't likely to run into any experts around here," Blannon said. Then he grinned. "Besides, all you have to do is *act* like an expert. If someone asks you a technical question, rattle off some gibberish and look at them like they're stupid for asking. Nothing discourages people like being made to feel like a fool."

Easy for Blannon to say, Erek thought as he stood outside the open door with his heart pounding and sweat trickling inside the collar of his shirt. Blannon had told him to act confident, but how could he do that when he was sure this venture would be a dismal failure?

He'd almost convinced himself to turn back when he heard the faint swish of the door at the far end of the corridor. His mind conjured up a vision of how he must look standing uncertainly in front of the CommSec office—and that was enough to make him step quickly through the open doorway.

The office was smaller than he had expected—no more than five meters square. Four commsets were lined up along the far wall. A single curved monitor screen above the commsets showed a complex pattern of overlapping diagrams in bright green over a darker rectangular grid of lines. Behind each commset was a desk unit with an individual keyboard and readout screen.

Only the commset directly under the curved screen had an attached power unit giving it interstream functions. The others were used for ship's communications and interbase radio transmissions within the local zone.

A large, black-skinned Guard officer wearing a headset worked at the interstream commset, while a shabby-looking man in brown fatigues sat hunched over one of the desk units, pecking slowly at a keyboard. Both men were absorbed in their work; they hadn't heard Erek come in. He could still leave, and they would never know he'd been there. His eyes went to the sidearm strapped to the belt of the man at the desk unit.

You heard what Troy said . . .

The Guard officer swiveled around to reach for something on the workbench behind him and spotted Erek. His brow lifted in surprise. He pushed up the headset and said, "Who are you?"

Erek's throat went dry when he saw the interlocking pattern of silver rings at the man's collar. The man was a sergeant in the technical corps. Not a stasis tech—they were in a different service altogether. But the sergeant would have more than casual familiarity with sector ship stasis control. The story Erek and Gillie had put together crumbled under an instant surge of panic as Erek realized that the man wouldn't buy a song-and-dance that didn't make technical sense.

"Well?"

"I . . . ah . . . " Erek wet his lips with his tongue. "I—"

"Jensen must've sent him over to fix number four,"

said the other man, swiveling around and leaning back in his chair to regard Erek. He was seedy-looking even for a brig, with a birdlike face, long nose, pointed chin, and narrow mouth. "Said he might have somebody take a look at that tracking problem."

"Oh, yeah." The sergeant pushed back his chair and stood up, and something about his face made the knot of tension inside Erek ease a little. He was a huge man with bearlike shoulders and thick, muscular arms. But when he smiled he showed a mouthful of strong, white teeth against the dark skin, and his face became open and friendly. He did not have the stern bearing or veiled eyes of the Guard's security personnel.

Nor, Erek hoped, did he have the naturally suspicious mind.

"Scott Griffin." The officer extended a hand the size of a dinner plate across the workbench.

Erek stepped forward to shake his hand. He hadn't thought to make up a name, so he didn't offer one.

"No need to be so jumpy," the sergeant said with a smile. "We don't bite." He looked with open distaste at the other man and amended in a low voice: "Well, *I* don't, anyway. Think you can fix the unit in time for the skip?"

Erek felt a jolt of surprise. *In time for the skip.* He forced himself to keep his face expressionless. "I'll try, sir."

The man's teeth flashed again. "No 'sir's' around here. We aren't that formal anymore." Then his mouth turned down slightly as something else occurred to him. "I thought Colonel Cassady issued orders that all stasis techs were to remain on the flight deck."

"Well . . . " The small measure of confidence evaporated. "They said this was a rush job—"

The monitor behind the officer buzzed. Turning, he waved a hand at Erek. "Go ahead, then. Let me know if you need anything." He sat down at the console and pulled the headset over his ears.

"It's that one over there," said the other man, pointing at the commset against the far wall. "It gives us funny lines on the screen when we disconnect from the main computer. Been trying to get 'em to fix it since yesterday."

Feeling shaky, Erek stepped across to the unit, swiveled the chair around, and sat down. He sucked in air, let it out slowly. The 'set was activated and a single word hung in the center of the readout screen:

READY . . .

He sat there staring at it, but his mind was on what the black sergeant had said: *Think you can fix the unit in time for the skip?*

Was Cassady getting ready to take *Copernicus* on a long-distance skip sequence?

Erek shook his head. That wasn't his concern. He had come here for one reason. He had to yank the cable and get out of here as quickly as possible.

The unit in front of him wasn't an interstream commset, but according to Gillie the cable would work just as well with his 'set in the basement. Gillie had given him detailed instructions about how to disconnect the cable. He shouldn't have any trouble with that. But Erek knew that even the easygoing sergeant might get suspicious if he merely pulled out the cable and left. He would have to stall for a few minutes and act as if he were looking for the problem. Then maybe he could convince the sergeant that the cable was bad, and he would have to take it back to the shop to fix it.

He slid the chair forward on its track and looked over the commset. Whoever had last worked here hadn't been neat. The console shelf was stained with spilled jo and the fine dust of uncoated datachips. Papers overflowed the trash bin beside it. A dirty jo mug sat on the lower shelf next to the intercom handset. Beside the handset somebody had taped a small square of paper filled with handwritten names and numbers—probably ship's intercom codes.

But there were no clues about how to operate the commset. Erek's job as a streamer pilot called for use of standard interstream commsets, and most of the principles would carry over. But this 'set was designed to be used either as a stand-alone unit or in conjunction with other ship's systems, and many of the controls were unfamiliar to him.

He glanced over his shoulder. The sergeant saw him and gave a friendly wave. A few more minutes, Erek decided, turning back to the keyboard, then he would unplug the cable and get out of here.

The SYS DISCON key was in the lower left of the control pad. He pressed it, and wavy lines replaced the READY as contact with the ship's main switching computer was broken. He rotated the tracker ball at the side of the console, and the wavy lines skewed to the right. He tapped a few control keys, then rotated the ball again. The lines twisted to the left this time. He flipped off the power switch, then flipped it back on. The READY signal reappeared. The switch beside the master power toggle was an unfamiliar one labeled MOD. Erek pressed it experimentally.

"Griffin says the modulator won't do nothing unless you're running a spec program."

Erek jumped, and quickly glanced sideways to find the thin man watching him.

"Didn't you know that?"

Erek forced himself to stay calm. The man knew some of the terminology, which meant he'd been given some training. But Erek was willing to bet that the training was minimal. Blannon's advice came back to him:

Rattle off some gibberish and look at them like they're stupid for asking . . .

"Sometimes a bad modulator will show up on the

screen during warm-up," he said. "Didn't *you* know that?"

The man stared at him a moment longer, then grunted and turned back to his work.

Erek fiddled with the keypad a few minutes to give his nerves time to settle down. Then he turned again to look behind him. The sergeant had swiveled back to his console; Erek could see lines of data flowing across the curved screen. The other man was hunched over his keyboard.

Erek got up as quietly as possible and stepped around to look at the back of the commset. The interface cable was connected to the wall unit with a simple plug, and went through a small cut-out in the rear panel exactly as Gillie had described. Erek squatted down on his heels and studied the panel's latching mechanism. He reached out to open it. Then he heard a sound, jerked around, and almost collided with the big sergeant.

"Didn't mean to startle you," Griffin said with a grin. "Any luck?"

Erek tried to say something, but garbled it in his momentary panic. He waved toward the panel and found some words. "I was getting ready to check the connections in the back here."

Griffin nodded, but didn't seem very interested in Erek's explanation. He glanced at the other man who still worked at the desk unit with his back to them. His nose wrinkled slightly. Then he leaned closer to Erek and whispered: "Make sure you get back to the flight deck before the skip window opens. We'll have people there to watch out for you in case the brigs try anything funny."

Before Erek could think of a reply, the sergeant clapped him on the shoulder, turned, and lumbered back to his commset. Erek's eyes followed him. *What is happening on this ship?*

Erek shook his head. He had to keep his mind on his main goal. He could unsnap the cable and be out of here in thirty seconds. That was none too soon as far as he was concerned. He twisted the latch to let the panel fall open.

Then he hesitated again. If Cassady were getting ready to take *Copernicus* through the stream, it would help to know where he was going, and how soon. Even if Gillie's commset punched a message to that post on Semegen IV, it would take the Guard a few hours to organize a rescue effort. The ship could be gone before they arrived.

Erek craned his neck to look over the top of the commset unit. He couldn't come right out and ask; the sergeant had acted as if Erek already knew about the skip. So how could he find out—

Then it hit him.

Leaving the service panel open, he came slowly to his feet and stepped back around to the front of the commset, his eyes studying the readout screen.

READY...

If Cassady were setting up a skip, the ship's main stasis computers would know about it. Putting a starship the size of *Copernicus* through a skip involved dozens of major computer systems. The target coordinates had to be set well in advance, and onboard commsets throughout the ship had to have access to those coordinates in order to calculate the transmission frequencies. If Erek could get into the stasis control system, it should be easy to ask for the destination coordinates.

He licked his lips and glanced behind him. The sergeant was absorbed in his work at the interstream unit. The other man was still hunched over the work station with his back to Erek.

Erek swiveled the chair and sat down. He checked behind him once more, then flipped back the keyboard cover and entered a command:

QUERY

The screen blinked and lighted with a response:

MAINLINE CONNECT
READY FOR QUERY REFERENCE . . .

Erek keyed:

STASIS SYSTEM

The computer came back with:

STASIS SYSTEM INTERRUPT—
ENTER ACCESS CODE . . .

He should have expected a security lock. He thought for a moment, his fingertips resting on the keys. Then, lacking anything better, he entered a random four-digit number. The computer kicked it out immediately and repeated the request. He tried again with the same result. Sweat dripped from his chin onto the keyboard. He wiped it off, glanced over his shoulder at the sergeant, turned back to the screen. He pursed his lips, inhaled, blew out.

Then his eyes went to the white square of paper that was taped to the console shelf. Most of the numbers had names scribbled next to them. He was sure they were intercom codes. Troy's men would be unfamiliar with the ship's intercom system, and it made sense that they would write down the codes they used most frequently and keep them close to the handset for easy reference. But there was another number at the bottom of the paper that was too long to be an intercom code. Erek reached up with an index finger to touch the paper just below the longer series of digits. It also stood to reason that those men would be unfamiliar with the computer's security codes . . .

He keyed in the series of numbers and held his breath. The computer responded immediately:

> *STASIS SYSTEM QUERY*
> *PLEASE ENTER DATABASE*
> *CHARACTERISTICS . . .*

He released the breath. So far, so good. But getting past the security system was only the first step. Now he would have to feel his way through the inquiry. He entered:

STASIS CONTROL SYSTEM DRIVE LINK

The computer responded:

> *DO YOU WANT FULL HP-150 SCAN ON*
> *STASIS/DRIVE COORDINATION?*

That didn't sound right. He keyed a negative reply and the computer took him back to the stasis command level. He tried again:

QUERY STASIS/DRIVE COORDINATION
LIMITED SCAN

The computer's response was:

> *ENTER SCAN PARAMETERS . . .*

Erek had no idea what that meant. He felt sweat beading on his forehead. He wiped it off with the back of his arm and keyed:

RETURN TO BASE STASIS SYSTEM
READY . . .

Then he entered the command that was universal for any computer system that interacted with humans:

HELP

That got an immediate response:

DO YOU WANT QUERY ASSISTANCE INTO STASIS SYSTEM?

YES

PROCEED WITH REQUEST . . .

That wasn't much help. He thought some more and keyed:

CATALOG HELP

The computer responded with a stream of catalog entries that scrolled across the screen at a pace too fast to follow. He pressed the pause key and reviewed a screenful of data that meant nothing to him. He glanced over his shoulder again. The men were still busy, but he knew it would only be a matter of time before one of them looked over to see what he was doing. Trying to explain a query to the stasis computer would be touchy, to say the least.

He chewed his lower lip, thinking. Then he cleared the screen and entered a new command:

QUERY DRIVE SYSTEM SKIP DESTINATION

The computer responded with:

STASIS/DRIVE LINK
PROCEED WITH QUERY . . .

Erek entered:

SKIP DESTINATION

The answer flashed immediately:

DESTINATION FOR DRIVE SYSTEM
COORDINATES 3KX-91499 AND 7RN-
85099 . . .

He frowned at the double set of coordinates. Then he
entered:

QUERY COMMON NAME FOR COORDINATES
3KX-91499 AND 7RN-85099

The computer replied:

STAGE-TWO PLANET KNOWN AS KISATCHIE . . .

Chapter 7

THEY left the stairwell on the fourth level and ducked into a videodome to catch their breath. Erek would have preferred to keep moving until they reached the safety of the basement, but Leo Blannon was red-faced and panting from the heat and unaccustomed exertion, and even Erek had to admit that it felt good to let himself sink into one of the deep-cushioned viewing chairs.

Blannon eased himself into the chair beside him with a heavy sigh. Gillie hunkered down on his heels in the wide aisle that separated their seats from the row in front. Joby and Richard took sentry positions near the door.

"What happened?" Blannon asked.

Erek kept the summary brief and to the point. When he described how he'd gotten past the main computer's security system, Gillie chuckled appreciatively.

"Doesn't surprise me. Programmers come up with all kinds of schemes to keep people out of restricted areas, then operators write down the code numbers and leave them where anyone can find them."

Blannon clapped Erek on the back. "We'll make a reporter out of you yet!" Then his brow furrowed. "Kisatchie. Rings a bell, but . . . " He gazed out at the dome, thinking. Then he shook his head. "Can't place it. Any idea where it's at?"

"All I could get was the name. Nothing else."

"How come?"

"The information was shielded. I don't know why, unless Cassady doesn't want the stasis techs to find out where he's taking the ship."

Gillie was more interested in the interface cable that lay coiled in his hand. "It's exactly what I need. Now we'll be able to call that Guard post without any trouble."

Getting the cable out of the CommSec office turned out to be easier than Erek had expected. Sergeant Griffin merely waved from his commset when Erek made his pitch about taking the cable back to the shop for repairs. He disconnected the cable following Gillie's directions, then left the office and stepped across the corridor to the storage cubby. The sergeant would be expecting him to return in an hour or so with the cable, and would probably try to find out what had happened to him. But by that time Erek and the others would have long since reached the basement.

"You're sure about the skip time?" Blannon asked.

"Tomorrow at oh-nine hundred," Erek told him. "That's when the next window opens. The skip sequence has already started."

Blannon frowned down at his wristwatch. He switched the still-unlighted cheroot from one corner of his mouth to the other and kept silent.

Something was on Blannon's mind, but Erek felt too tired and drained by the heat to wonder about it. He looked out at the holographic image of the videodome. On standby, the dome reflected a peaceful scene of a sprawling, open-air city—what one might expect to see from a nearby hilltop. The buildings, square blocks of brown and tan, were separated by patches of blue-green vegetation. White spires curved toward the pale blue sky. From the style, Erek guessed the city was an early Omegan settlement from a hundred years or so ago. In the background glimmered a vast blue body of water.

He let his head fall back against the padded headrest and closed his eyes. Maybe he would wake up and find that all this was a bad dream—

Beep.

Erek spun around, coming half out of his chair. Then he saw that Blannon had taken his notepad out and flipped it open.

"Query, Kisatchie," Blannon said.

The pad beeped again, a different tone this time as it accepted Blannon's voiceprint. It took a moment to sort through its library, then said:

"Query reference, primary data check on K. Satchy, full name Kenneth Maxwell Satchy, third governor on—"

"No, no," Blannon interrupted. "Kisatchie." He spelled it out. The machine thought for a moment, then intoned: "Query, Kisatchie, reduced on positive reference search to twelve possible locates." The voice came out of the tiny speaker grille in singsong tones of neutral gender. The sound of a notepad always set Erek's nerves on edge. "Verbal response will require three point one eight standard hours. Hard-copy printout is recommended."

"We don't have a printer," Blannon said.

Inferring no query, the notepad remained silent.

"Ask it for major keys on the sort," Erek suggested. "That should narrow it down." He allowed his body to sink back into the chair. He felt bone-weary with the heat and the tension of the past ten hours, and the beginning of a headache drummed at the back of his skull. He didn't know what Blannon was trying to accomplish, but he hoped he would get it over with as quickly as possible so they could go back to the basement.

Blannon repeated Erek's request to the notepad.

"Major keys are Historical Sites—three referents with fifty-three subcategories; Persons, Living—nine referents with twenty subcategories; Persons, Deceased —three referents with fifty subcategories; Planetary Names—one referent with sixteen subcategories—"

"That's it," Erek said.

"Query, Planetary Names," Blannon said, interrupting the notepad. "General Survey."

The pad's response was immediate:

"Kisatchie is a developed planet in the Lietz Sector of Quadrant Ninety-eight in local star cluster Omega Centauri. Subject planet is a stream focal point defined by coordinate locations 3KX-91499 and 7RN-85099. Initial landing and coordinate tracks were made at date 33.92 GCC by Explorer Captain Carlos Dahl, operating under contract with Deep Space Administration coordinated through the starship *Applegate*. Current file on subject planet includes information about limited scope Guard posts under construction at two local sites—"

"Tell me about development," Blannon cut in.

"Query assumption: Reference to planetary development as it pertains to previous query, or to development of specific planetary unit known as Kisatchie, or to general terminology definition? Please clarify."

Blannon made a sound in his throat and tried again. "I want to know what Kisatchie is like. Tell me about development and colonization."

"First planetary development of Kisatchie began on 33.98 GCC," the notepad said, and fell silent.

"Current status?" Blannon prompted.

"Query, please clarify."

"I want to know the current status of Kisatchie."

"Reference query, please clarify subject component of question."

Blannon stared helplessly at the notepad. Beside him, Gillie chuckled. Erek had always thought it strange that

Leo Blannon, who was so skillful at drawing information out of uncooperative people, had such difficulty getting simple answers from his notepad's database.

"Tell it you want the current status of planetary development efforts on Kisatchie," he suggested. He would have conducted the inquiry himself, but the pad's microprocessor would respond only to Blannon's voiceprint.

Blannon relayed the question tersely.

"Kisatchie development is currently at stage two," the notepad answered. "Stage-three development began at date 34.09 GCC and was canceled by official Omega Command order on 34.12 GCC."

Blannon frowned. "Canceled? That's odd."

"Query reference to—"

"I wasn't talking to you," Blannon growled. The notepad fell silent. Blannon looked up at Erek. "Ever hear of UNSA abandoning a planet once development was started?"

Erek shook his head. Despite the far reaches given to humankind via the k-stream, the discovery of habitable worlds over the past three centuries of exploration had been few and far between. It wasn't like UNSA to waste one. "Maybe they didn't abandon it. Ask for the principal industry."

Blannon passed along the request. The notepad answered promptly: "Penal colony."

Blannon snapped his fingers. "That's it! I knew there was something familiar about that name." He folded the notepad and slipped it into his pocket. "Maximum security. One of the first colonies in Omega."

Gillie had a puzzled look on his face. "They have whole planets that are prisons?"

"Not many," Blannon told him. "And they only put the hardcores there. Mostly brigs. The Guard turns the planet over to them, with a few fortified outposts to keep track of what's going on."

"Why would Cassady want to take the ship to a place like that?"

"Good question," Blannon said. "Whatever his plans are, they call for heavy firepower. He's got the *Wasp*, and those powerguns he installed on *Copernicus*. Makes you wonder who he'll be coming up against."

"If he's going to a penal colony," Erek said, "he'll be facing some strong security forces—" His words broke off suddenly. He and Blannon stared at one another. Gillie finally voiced what all three of them were thinking:

"Breakout?"

"Couldn't be." Erek shook his head firmly. "Even Cassady wouldn't be that crazy."

"He's got enough guns to do it," Blannon said. "Especially with the *Wasp*'s interstream missiles."

Erek shook his head from side to side. "When you plan a prison break, you do it to get somebody out. Cassady's been in the Guard for twenty years. You said yourself that until now he's had a clean record. Why would he want to break anyone out of a penal colony?"

"Hey," Joby called from the door. "How long you gonna sit there gabbing?"

"We'll go in a minute," Gillie told her. Then he turned back to Blannon. "Your notepad said something about that planet being a focal point. And it gave two different sets of coordinates. I thought any location in the stream could be defined by a single set."

"You're right." Blannon raised an inquiring eyebrow at Erek.

"A focal point is a mass-plus on the border between two stream zones," Erek furnished. "That should have tipped me off right away. All the planetary penal colonies were established at focal points. Makes security easier."

"How so?" Blannon asked.

"The only way in and out of a focal point is through a

combination set of coordinates that covers both zones."

Gillie looked puzzled. "A focal point can be a planet?"

"Sure. Or a star. Or a sector ship for that matter, just like any other stream location."

Gillie had another question half out of his mouth when Blannon interrupted:

"Unfortunately, that isn't pertinent to our problem. Now that we know where Cassady wants to take the ship, we have to figure out how to stop him."

Erek looked up sharply. "We have to do *what?*"

"Stop Cassady from taking *Copernicus* through that skip window. Maybe we can—"

"Wait a minute," Erek interrupted. "We came up here to call the Guard." He nodded toward the cable in Gillie's hand. "Now we can do that. We can't stop Cassady, but the Guard can. That's their job."

"But what if they don't get here in time?" Blannon tapped his wristwatch. "The skip window will open in six hours. It'll take us at least an hour to get back to the basement and fire up Gillie's commset. That means the Guard will only have five hours to get organized and skip out here."

"So? All they have to do is get a priority channel and set up a coordinated skip sequence."

Blannon shook his head stubbornly. "They have to get authorization first. That might not be so easy with forty stasis techs still aboard the ship."

"What's that got to do with it? If anything, it should make them want to get here as fast as possible."

Blannon grunted. "Bureaucrats like to make sure their hindquarters are covered before they deal with touchy situations. A hijacked sector ship complete with hostages definitely qualifies as a touchy situation."

"Yeah, but that's—"

"The Guard commander on Semegen IV won't send a squad out here without getting approval from his superiors at Omega Command. They'll want to make sure somebody higher up signs off before they give the okay. By the time anyone has the guts to make a decision, Cassady will have already skipped."

"What's wrong with that?" Erek asked. "That's why I got the skip destination coordinates—so we could pass them along to the Guard. They'll know where to find us."

"That'll help," Blannon said, but not in a way that conceded the argument. "But there's something else bothering me. You said the sergeant at the CommSec office told you to get back to the flight deck before the window opens. Said you'd be safer there?"

"Something like that. But—"

"Sounds like things could get messy after the skip. If Cassady's planning on using all those guns against the security force at that penal colony, I can see why. Be a lot better if we could keep him here."

That part made sense. With the *Wasp*'s interstream missiles, Cassady could strike a target from several skip-zones away—well out of range of the penal colony's conventional weapons. Messy situation, like Blannon said. Lots of people killed. But that didn't change the facts.

"There's only five of us," Erek pointed out. "We aren't exactly experts in guerrilla warfare. There's no way we can go up against fourteen renegade guardsmen and several dozen armed brigs."

"I was thinking more of sabotage than brute force," Blannon said. He pushed himself out of the chair and began pacing the aisle. "Something we can do without any risk at all."

Erek rolled his eyes. "I've heard that before . . . "

"We passed some computer consoles in the basement. Relay stations, too. Maybe we can use one of those to get into the ship's drive system and disable it. You're the expert in that area. Any possibilities?"

By referring to skip-sequencing a starship as *that area*, Blannon included a lot of ground that lay outside

Erek's experience as a Class IV streamer pilot. But Erek didn't have to be experienced in starship control to be certain of one thing.

"We won't be able to reach the drive system from any control station in the basement. System designers aren't that loose with drive security. Most of the control stations down there are for troubleshooting and maintenance."

Blannon made a clucking sound in his throat. "Can't we do *something* with 'em?"

"Maybe, if we tinkered with them long enough. But that'd be like throwing out a red flag. We'd almost surely draw a tech's attention on a monitor someplace."

"What about the solar panels?"

That came from Gillie. Erek and Blannon turned to look at him. Gillie's tone made it clear he had something in mind.

"Don't they have to be flat against the hull for a skip?"

Erek realized instantly what the boy meant. He explained it to Blannon. "Everything on the outside of the ship has to be retracted or folded down flat against the hull before a skip can be made. That includes the reflector panels." It was the same with landing struts and radio antennae on smaller streamers like the *Aire Vega*. The lesson had been learned the hard way during the early years of stream exploration; a physical projection on a ship entering the kohlmann stream could cause enough instability in the streamwave to pull a ship apart and scatter it across several light-years of space. Not even k-stream physicists knew why, but it was a fact that had to be lived with. Because of that, drive computers were programmed to abort a skip if all external mechanisms weren't retracted or folded down.

"What does that do for us?" Blannon still didn't see what Gillie was leading up to.

"The motor controls for the solar panels are in the basement," Gillie answered. "We passed some on the way up here. All we have to do is trace the circuits to one of the relay stations, then cut through a few cables. When Cassady orders the skip, the drive computer will send a message to stasis control to close the solar panels. If they won't close, the computer will abort the skip.''

"Won't Cassady just send somebody down to fix it?"

"If we disable the controls just before the window opens and the skip order is given, he won't have time."

"Sounds like you might have something." Blannon turned to Erek. "What about it?"

"Well . . . '' Gillie had already built up a lot of enthusiasm for his idea, and Erek didn't like to be the one to poke holes in it. But he had reservations. "Talking about it sounds good, but those control circuits will be protected. Solar panels are too important to take chances with circuit overloads and computer blips."

"You think we'd be better off going after the drive system?"

"Well, it'd be more of a sure thing, but . . . "

"I think you're right. Where would we have to go to find the right kind of console?"

"Flight deck, probably. But even if we got that far, we'd never be able to get into the drive system. Security's too tight."

"You did pretty well with the stasis computer," Blannon reminded him.

"That was nothing compared to what you're talking about. You have to know what you're doing to fool around with k-drive control."

"Hmmm." Blannon pursed his lips, thinking. Then: "Would a stasis technician be able to jam the drive system?"

"Probably. But they're—"

"Yeah, I know. They're all in the flight deck, too." Blannon nodded thoughtfully. "You're right. We'll have to go over there."

Chapter 8

JOBY stopped in front of a sealing door and studied the wall placard beside it. "We can go up here."

Without asking for Erek's concurrence, she twisted the dogs and pulled the door open. They stepped into a narrow, low-ceilinged passageway. Richard closed the door behind them and they followed the passage a few meters to another door that opened into a dimly lighted stairwell. Joby grasped the handrail and went up with Erek and Richard close behind.

Erek had been building up a bad case of the jitters ever since they left the videodome and returned to the basement. Working their way down the length of the cylinder to the other hub structure was part of Blannon's master plan, to which Erek had somehow agreed without realizing it. His mission, with assistance from Joby and Richard, was to contact one of the stasis techs and enlist his help in sabotaging the ship's drive control system. Meanwhile, Blannon and Gillie had gone back to the alcove in the basement to install the interface cable and make the call to Semegen IV. Then, as a backup in case Erek didn't succeed, Gillie would try to disable one of the solar panel controls to prevent it from closing down for the skip.

Erek felt that the last, and riskiest, part was unnecessary. But Blannon had argued that stopping Cassady from going through that stream window was too important to leave to chance. If they attacked from two directions, one of them would surely hit the mark.

Erek was even less enthusiastic about the plan after the sweaty, nerve-wracking trek through the basement. They had used up more than two hours getting here, and now they barely had three hours in which to make contact with a stasis technician before the window opened.

The only bright spot Erek could see was that by now Gillie had surely gotten his call out to Semegen IV. The Guard was probably already taking steps to assemble a rescue mission.

Erek stepped onto a stairwell landing, glanced up at the placard, and saw with surprise that they had already reached the third level. He asked Joby to stop. "Let's take a look outside."

She glanced up at him in mild surprise, then shrugged and stepped aside so he could open the door a crack. The corridor was empty and silent, the overhead lights dim. The numbered doors that lined both sides of the corridor were all shut. He closed the door and turned back to her. Richard leaned against the stairwell railing with his arms folded across his chest.

"I think you and Richard should wait here."

"How come? The flight deck's on the fifth level."

"I know. But Troy's men are probably quartered on the fourth. Guardsmen, too. That's only one floor above us." Erek fingered the sleeve of the black and gray uniform shirt he still wore. "By myself, I might be able to get up there without drawing too much attention. But if anyone sees you and Richard, there'll be trouble."

She grumbled about it, but eventually gave in. They found a nearby stateroom that looked as if it hadn't been used in a while.

"Keep the door locked," he said. "I shouldn't be gone long." He hesitated, then added, "If I'm not back in an hour, you and Richard go back to the outside hub."

"What if—"

"If I don't come back, it'll probably mean I slipped into the basement someplace else. I don't want to have to worry about coming back here for you two."

Erek left before she could argue. He fixed the stateroom number firmly in his mind and returned to the stairwell.

On the fifth level, he again cracked open the door. He had hoped to find a side passage with little traffic, but saw immediately that the corridor outside was one of the major arteries running the breadth of the hub structure. A burly Guard officer walked past, then another. A group of brigs coming from the opposite direction talked in low tones. Several other uniformed men stood near an open doorway a few meters away.

Erek's heart was beating too fast, and he could feel the perspiration start in his palms. *I'll have to get a grip on myself if I'm going to pull this off.*

The thought only made him feel more tense.

At last, nobody seemed to be looking in his direction. He opened the door quickly and slipped through. According to the placard on the wall, the flight deck was to the left. He hesitated only a moment, then turned and started walking. He kept his face averted when he walked past the group of brigs. He was aware of their eyes on him, and felt better after he'd gone a dozen meters farther down the corridor. Two guardsmen crossed in front of him without even looking in his direction. Another came toward him down the corridor.

Then Erek noticed a fundamental difference in both attitude and appearance between the guardsmen and the brigs. While Troy's men were unkempt and, for the most part, unwashed as well, the guardsmen all looked as neat and well-pressed as they must have looked during personnel inspection on the *Wasp*. They walked carefully erect while the brigs slouched about.

There was another basic difference. The brigs all *looked* like criminals, with shifty eyes and suspicious faces. But the black sergeant in the CommSec office had seemed pleasant enough, even friendly—not at all the sort to be involved in hijacking a sector ship.

But he *was* involved, Erek reminded himself. All the guardsmen were involved. He would have to remember that they were potentially dangerous regardless of how they looked and acted.

Suddenly he realized that the guardsman coming toward him was giving him an odd look. Erek turned his head away and walked quickly past. His heart went back into double time, and his legs tensed, ready to run. From the corner of his eye, he saw the man hesitate, then move on down the corridor.

Why had the man looked at him that way? There were forty stasis technicians aboard the ship. Not a lot, but enough so that a guardsman wouldn't be likely to know all their faces. Yet something had definitely drawn the man's attention.

Then Erek realized that he hadn't seen anyone else in the corridor wearing the diagonal crosshatch of the stasis technician. He remembered something the black sergeant had said:

I thought Colonel Cassady issued orders that all stasis techs were to stay on the flight deck.

Erek's step faltered, and he moved closer to the wall. He felt the weight of the pellet gun in his pocket, and immediately wished he'd left it in the stateroom with Joby and Richard. If he were stopped and questioned, and the weapon found . . .

He approached an intersection—another major corridor that branched both left and right. The sign on the wall indicated that another left turn would take him to the flight deck. With every nerve fiber screaming at him to turn and race back to the stairwell, he turned left.

He had gone less than twenty meters when the corridor widened into a large lobby. A message processing center with several desk consoles was built into a recessed niche on the right side. On the other side was the wide entrance to the flight deck, with the security doors folded back.

Erek slowed his pace and edged closer for a look inside. Almost immediately he saw uniforms with the familiar crosshatch. That was enough to decide the issue. He stepped quickly through the doors, then moved a few paces to the side where he could stand with his back to the wall and get his bearings.

Erek had been inside the flight deck of only one other sector ship. As far as he could see this one had the same basic design—a vast round room with three circular tiers of work stations. He had come through an entrance to the second tier. A narrow aisle with a metal railing circled the perimeter. Spaced at irregular intervals along the aisle were breaks between the work stations, with short passages that led outward to administrative offices, washrooms, and other support facilities.

The command module, with a captain's chair and three-sided control panel, was in the center of the lower level at a location from which the ranking officer could see every activity in the room. Erek was relieved to see that the captain's chair was empty; in practice, he knew that starship captains spent most of their time in their private offices, and rarely visited the flight deck.

Fewer than a third of the work stations were occupied, but as far as Erek could see, all the operators wore uniforms with the crosshatch pattern. At least his tunic wouldn't draw attention in here. A dozen of Troy's brigs lounged about, mostly around the command module. They didn't seem to be doing much more than talking among themselves. Probably here to keep an eye

on the stasis techs, he decided. There were no guardsmen that he could see.

The presence of the brigs would make his task more
difficult; if he hoped to pull off Blannon's grand
scheme, he knew he would have to find a stasis technician who was isolated enough for a few minutes of private conversation.

His eyes searched again, and this time he found what
he needed—a woman working alone at a console almost
directly across from him. At least ten meters separated
her from the next occupied console.

He squared his shoulders, trying to pump himself up
with confidence, and started along the curving aisle. He
kept his face averted when he passed occupied work stations; he wasn't sure how the stasis technicians would
react if they realized he didn't belong in their small
group. He could only hope they would have the
presence of mind to keep silent.

He stepped past one of the moving escalators connecting the three tiers, and on to the woman's work station a few paces beyond. He sat down at the station
beside her. From behind the cover of the readout screen,
he made another quick survey of the flight deck. As far
as he could see, his stroll around the perimeter had gone
unnoticed.

He looked over at the woman. She was younger than
he'd first thought, slender, with short brown hair and
wideset brown eyes. She gave him a single curious
glance and went back to her work.

"I'm Erek Speros—" he began softly.

"We can't talk," she whispered without looking at
him.

The terse statement puzzled him. There was nobody
within hearing distance. "Why not?"

"They watch us." She inclined her head toward the
lower tier. Erek realized she was referring to the group
of brigs standing around the command module.
"They'll come up if they see us talking. Turn on the

console and set it on local, then key three two eight.''

He turned to look at her. ''What—''

''Hit the local key, then three two eight.''

Perplexed, he reached to the side of the console and flipped the power switch. When the ready signal beeped, he keyed the combination she'd given him. Almost immediately, a line appeared on the screen:

WHO ARE YOU AND WHAT DO YOU WANT?

He glanced sideways at her, then leaned closer to the keyboard and tapped an answer:

MY NAME IS EREK SPEROS. I WORK FOR SPOTLIGHT NEWS. WE NEED YOUR HELP.

From the corner of his eye, he saw her give him a quick, inquiring glance. Using the keyboard, he gave her a brief account of how he and Leo Blannon had found *Copernicus*, and their encounter with Joby and the others. She was clearly puzzled by the existence of the three children in the basement, but seemed to accept his story readily enough. When he asked how much she knew of Cassady's plans, she replied:

DESTINATION IS SHIELDED. WINDOW WILL OPEN IN A FEW HOURS. BEYOND THAT, NOTHING. THEY ONLY TELL US ENOUGH TO DO OUR JOBS.

He hadn't really expected her to know much about that. He keyed:

WE'VE LEARNED THAT THE DESTINATION IS KISATCHIE. PENAL COLONY. DON'T KNOW WHY. WE'VE GOTTEN A MESSAGE TO THE GUARD. WE CAN'T LET CASSADY TAKE THE SHIP THROUGH THAT WINDOW. WE HAVE TO BUY ENOUGH TIME FOR THE GUARD TO GET HERE.

When she didn't answer right away, he looked over and found her watching him with disbelief. Then she turned back to her keyboard.

YOU CALLED THE GUARD POST ON SEM-EGEN IV?

At least she knew something of the local area. He replied:

YES. WE HAVE A COMMSET IN THE BASE-MENT.

Her eyes were on him again. She gave a puzzled shake of her head and keyed:

WHEN DID YOU CALL THEM?

Why was she having such a difficult time accepting his statement?

WITHIN THE PAST TWO HOURS. CAN YOU USE YOUR CONSOLE TO SABOTAGE THE DRIVE SYSTEM SO CASSADY WON'T BE ABLE TO TAKE THE SHIP THROUGH THE WINDOW?

She sat for a moment, staring at the screen. Then she keyed:

I'LL HAVE TO CHECK WITH SOMEONE ELSE. WAIT.

She touched the control key with one hand and tapped in another combination with the other. Erek's screen blanked. He kept his eyes on it while beside him the woman typed rapidly on her keyboard. He knew she was communicating with somebody—probably another stasis tech somewhere on the flight deck. She paused now and then, presumably to read a response before typing again.

After a few minutes of this, the screen in front of Erek blinked with a new message:

TOO LATE. SEQUENCE FOR THE SKIP STARTED SEVERAL HOURS AGO.

Erek stared at the words without moving. He couldn't accept the flat dismissal of the reason he had risked his life getting to the flight deck. He asked:

CAN'T YOU SHUT IT DOWN?

NOT FROM HERE. ONLY POSSIBLE TO DO THAT FROM EMERGENCY COMMAND MODULE. BUT WE CAN'T GET IN THERE. IT'S UNDER GUARD.

Erek glanced at the chronometer inset in the corner of the readout screen. A little over two hours remained before the skip window would open. If only there were some way to reach Blannon, to find out if he and Gillie had succeeded in jamming the solar panel.

He reached for the keyboard to ask about the emergency command module, but before he could complete the question, a sound from below caught his attention. He looked past the readout screen and saw several of the men on the lower tier staring up at him. Three of them had stepped on the escalator and were headed for the second tier. They carried handguns.

Erek didn't take the time to wonder what had tipped them off. He swiveled around and left the chair in a crouching run. Keeping his head below the top level of the railing, he ran down the aisle toward a stairway entrance he remembered passing on his way up here. The escalator was just past it. The men spotted him and began taking the steps two at a time.

When he realized he wouldn't be able to beat them to the stairway entrance, he spun around and started running back toward the work station he'd left. Several meters past it another aisle branched off and led to an open doorway in the back wall of the flight deck. Erek had no idea where that would take him, but it was his only option. He cut away to head for the doorway on a more direct route, dodging around work stations and startled technicians. He'd almost reached the opening when he heard a shouted order behind him.

He forced more speed out of his legs. His knee cracked against the corner of a work station, and a sharp pain shot up his leg. He ignored it. If he could reach that doorway—

Then something exploded against the back of his neck, and everything went black.

Chapter 9

"WHOOEEE!" Blannon said, mopping his brow. "Sure is hot. How much longer will that take?"

"Almost done." Gillie held something in his hand that looked to Blannon like a tiny doughnut with wires. He plugged it into the back of the commset's processor unit, checking carefully to make sure all the pins were seated. Then he reached to the tray beside him for another wire doughnut. "We'll be ready to give it a try in a few minutes."

"Great!" Blannon clapped the boy on the shoulder. "Now we're getting somewhere!"

Gillie gave him a self-conscious grin. "Hope so."

Installing the cable Erek had taken from the Comm-Sec office was turning into more of a project than Blannon had expected. Gillie had been working steadily for the better part of an hour under the dim glow of the lantern, taking apart the processor and putting it back together. The cable itself was no problem—it had a simple plug at each end that even Blannon with his ten thumbs might have been able to connect. But, as Gillie explained it, when he originally assembled the 'set, he'd modified it so it would operate—although with limited functions—without the interface cable. Now he had to reverse those modifications.

Blannon had watched as the boy fastened electrical connections with paperclips and scraps of wire and other paraphernalia he'd scavenged from the basement —and kept to himself the doubts about whether the makeshift contraption would ever be able to punch a call through to Semegen IV. The boy seemed confident, but . . .

Blannon thrust his hands into the pockets of his slacks and wandered out to the corridor to stand in the doorway that was formed by the stacked crates. The corridor was dark, and silent except for the distant drone of a ventilating fan. He didn't know what he was looking for; it was too soon to expect Erek and the others to be coming back, and Gillie had assured him that neither Cassady's guardsmen nor Troy's brigs ever came to this part of the basement.

He sighed and fished the notepad out of his pocket. If he was going to be stuck here, he might as well try to accomplish something. He flipped open the pad and said, "It's me."

The notepad matched Blannon's voiceprint and beeped a ready signal.

"We're going to try again," Blannon told it. "Give me more information about Victor Troy."

"Query, reference, Victor Troy subject as discussed previously or unrelated query."

"Reference subject as discussed previously," Blannon said.

In the weeks following the hijacking, many theories had been expounded to explain why Xavier Cassady had taken *Copernicus*, and enough information had been written about him to fill several dozen data chips. Along with every other reporter who had an interest in the story, Blannon had read everything he could get his hands on, and he had found nothing that could offer a clue to Cassady's motives. As far as he knew, neither had anyone else.

But now Blannon had some information that none of the other reporters could have guessed: Victor Troy was involved. That shed an entirely new light on the questions surrounding the hijacking.

Blannon had already come to the conclusion that Victor Troy was using heavy leverage on Xavier Cassady. That was the only reason a man of Cassady's caliber would have teamed up with a lizard like Troy. As far as Blannon could tell from the information his notepad had already given him, Cassady had never come in contact with Troy on an official basis. Contrary to Blannon's first suspicions, Cassady had not been involved in the breakup of Troy's brig organization.

There had to be a common thread that connected the two men. Something that gave Troy a headlock on Cassady. If Blannon could find that thread, he was sure it would take him a long way toward finding out why Cassady had hijacked *Copernicus* in the first place.

"Victor Troy, reference: Criminal activities in recent Omegan history, Markos Sector, 33.25 GC," the notepad was saying in its singsong tones. "Reference: Guard activities pursuant to local instability in Vail Sector, 34.74 GC. Reference: Smuggling activities of blacklist merchandise, general nature, between Malachi Sector and world governments of the Pallain Bloc, 35.09 GC. Reference: Association with individuals Jock Clyatt and Emil Troy in establishing piracy operations in traffic zones surrounding—"

"We've been through all that," Blannon interrupted. "I want to know about his earlier background."

"Victor Troy, reference search abort, insufficient search format."

Blannon mopped his brow. "Give me information about Victor Troy's background prior to earliest recorded crimes." Maybe the connecting thread went back farther than he'd first thought.

"Earliest recorded crimes, reference dates precede Victor Troy's birth by approximately seven thousand standard years."

Blannon pondered, then amended the query: "Give me information about Victor Troy's background prior to *Victor Troy's* earliest recorded crimes."

"Query, reference, search response results in no available information."

Blannon took a deep breath. Dead end.

Then something else occurred to him. Maybe he'd been concentrating too much on looking for a link between Cassady and Troy. Troy and his brother had had a big organization—the most widespread brig operation in Omega before the Guard shut them down. His brother was Emil Troy, and the pad had mentioned another name . . .

"Query," he said to the notepad. "Guard files on individuals Jock Clyatt and Emil Troy."

"Jock Clyatt and Emil Troy, reference parallel: Known business associates of Victor Troy. Emil Troy sibling-related."

Business associates? Whoever had entered that piece of data must have had a wry sense of humor. "Query, subject background on limit of three standard years."

"Jock Clyatt and Emil Troy significant entries— Guard fugitives wanted for leading raids on nine semi-developed planets on the Omega Fringe, specifically the planets of Sandor, Char'd'Sun, Giant Forest, Indland, Briar—"

"Forget that," Blannon interrupted. "Parallel search, Jock Clyatt, Emil Troy, Xavier Cassady."

That took a few seconds. Then:

"No parallel, subject query."

Blannon shook his head, trying to capture a thought he sensed lurking just beyond his awareness. It wouldn't come to him.

"We're almost ready to give it a try," Gillie called.

Blannon closed the notepad and slipped it into his pocket. In the alcove, Gillie had moved the keyboard around to prop it against the front of the processor unit. The processor itself rested on top of a metalfilm crate with its circuit boards and bubble chips exposed. The readout screen was propped on another crate, and the cabling that connected the two units was strung loosely across the floor.

This haphazard assembly was supposed to punch a message across three stream zones to Semegen IV?

When Gillie switched on the 'set, the cooling fan at the back came to life with a faint hum, and the screen lighted with a blurred but readable message:

DIRECTORY EMPTY—ENTER TRANSMISSION COORDINATES . . .

Gillie reached into the side of the terminal box and twisted something that made the image of the words clearer.

"Directory empty," Blannon read. "What's that mean?"

"Nothing serious." Gillie positioned the keyboard in front of him and tapped in a set of instructions. "I'll have to enter the setup string manually. That's standard procedure when you start from scratch."

"What's a setup string?"

"Destination coordinates for the message."

"Oh." Then: "Do you know the coordinates of that Guard post?"

Gillie shook his head. "We'll have to try random sets, and watch the sequence patterns for convergence. That isn't the best way, but we'll hit it eventually."

"Eventually?"

Gillie began entering numbers into the keypad. The lines on the readout screen formed changing patterns. Blannon leaned against a nearby crate and watched.

Half an hour had crawled by when Gillie keyed in a number and pressed the ENTER key, and the lines jumped and formed a crisscross pattern Blannon hadn't seen before. He leaned forward expectantly.

"Is that the pattern you were talking about?"

Gillie hunched his shoulders slightly without answering. Blannon bit down on his lower lip and forced himself to keep quiet while the boy worked with the cluster of control keys, watching the screen intently. The pattern went away, and another one took its place.

"How can you tell anything from—"

Blannon's words were interrupted by a loud squawk from the commset's speaker box.

"*All right!*" Gillie said excitedly. "Here we go."

The commset beeped and a short message appeared at the bottom of the readout screen:

CONNECTION—COORDINATES 6RX-50499 MASS-PLUS LOCATION PLANET SEMEGEN IV UNITED NATIONS SPACE ADMINISTRA- TION BASE UNIT 6RX-504-KN32 CONFIRM . . .

Gillie punched in a reply so quickly it scrolled across the screen and vanished before Blannon had a chance to read it.

"Give it a try." Gillie pointed to the palm-size microphone that lay on the crate beside the processor unit. It was connected to the unit by a naked strand of silver wire. "There's no automatic voice activation, so you'll have to push the button there on the side."

Blannon picked up the microphone, careful of the wire. Then he hesitated. "Do I have to give call letters or anything?"

"Not that I know of. Anyway, we don't have any."

"No need to get fancy, I suppose." Blannon spoke into the slotted grille: "Hello? Can anybody hear me?"

"The button on the side," Gillie reminded him.

"Oh, yeah." Blannon pushed the button and tried again. "This is Leo Blannon. Is anybody picking this up?"

When he released the button, a roar of static burst from the speaker box, followed by a faint sound that may have been a voice.

"Keep trying," Gillie said, intently watching the lines on the screen while he punched the control keys. The lines crisscrossed, separated, wavered back and forth.

"This is Leo Blannon, with Spotlight News Service. Can you hear me? Over."

A male voice emerged from the static with sudden startling clarity:

" . . . station thirty-four in quadrant . . . . . . report specs through to NavSec HQ on . . . . . . transmission status is . . . "

"What's that mean?" Blannon asked. "Are they talking to us?"

"I don't think so. There's too much stream interference. We'll have to give it more power."

Something in the boy's voice made Blannon turn to look at him. "Any problem with that?"

"We'll blow the booster relay if we try to give it too much. It's already weak from the calls we made earlier." Gillie reached inside the front of the unit and made an adjustment. "Try it again."

Blannon pushed the button. "Mayday, mayday. This is Leo Blannon aboard *Copernicus*. We need help. Can anybody hear me?"

He waited through another burst of static. Then a new voice came through: " . . . pick up mayday without assigned coord . . . run it through for full scan . . . "

"They've got us!" Gillie exclaimed. "Give them our coordinates."

Erek had written *Copernicus*'s stream location coordinates on a scrap of paper. Blannon fished it out of his shirt pocket, unfolded it with one hand, and read the numbers. When he asked for confirmation, he was greeted only with static. "Can't you make it stronger?"

"I'm trying." Gillie keyed in a command and waited as the lines merged and separated several times in rapid succession. "We have to be careful or we'll—"

Something snapped in the back of the commset and the screen went blank.

"—burn that booster relay."

Chapter 10

AWARENESS came slowly to Erek. He lay on his back with his arms down along his sides. Light above him was bright enough to burn through his closed eyelids. His mind furnished a scenario: his apartment on Fynnland, city of Riis. Early morning, still in bed, sunlight washing across his face from the window.

He tried to roll away from the light. Something held him . . .

The memory returned in fragments, parts of a dream firming to reality. *Copernicus*. The flight deck. Troy's men . . .

He opened his eyes, turned his head, and froze as pain stabbed upward from his neck through his skull. A door opened nearby. He remained motionless. The door clicked shut. Footsteps approached.

"Excellent." He recognized the clipped voice of Victor Troy. "Did you find the others?"

Another voice, deeper, less refined: "Not yet. We'll get 'em, though."

The sharp edge of pain subsided to a throbbing ache in the back of his head. He knew that if he moved it would strike again.

"This one's awake," Troy said, his voice directly above Erek. "Where's Burdick?"

"On his way."

This one?

Erek opened his eyes slightly. Troy's face swam into view. Behind him stood a big man with a rugged face and gray-streaked beard. A dark patch of synthetic flesh covered one eye. Erek tried to move again, and realized he was stretched out on a narrow cot. Straps held him at wrists and ankles.

Troy watched him, his mouth fixed in a tight smile. Then his eyes flicked to something beside Erek. Erek turned his head slowly, gritting his teeth against another lancing pain. The brown-haired stasis technician was strapped to the cot beside him. She stared back at him, wide-eyed.

Erek tried to speak, coughed instead. His tongue was a slab of thick gristle, and his throat felt as if it were lined with steel barbs. They had used a stunbeam on him. Either that or he'd caught a reflected sizzler blast.

"Murph saw her talking to you," Troy explained. Erek moved his head enough to bring Troy back into view. Beside him, the bearded man grinned down at Erek with crooked teeth. Murph. The eye patch wrinkled obscenely—then Erek realized he was the man they had encountered on the tenth level, with the young Guard captain. He must have been with the other brigs near the command module on the flight deck.

Troy leaned close to Erek and his tone hardened. "What were you discussing with the technician?"

Erek swallowed. The light behind Troy was digging into his eyeballs. "Wanted to find out what you and Cassady planned to do with the ship," he said thickly. "Thought a stasis tech would know."

Troy's pale blue eyes remained steady, inches from

his own. "Where are the others?"

It took Erek a moment to understand who Troy was talking about. He groped for an answer, decided on a partial truth that he was sure wouldn't tell Troy anything he didn't already know:

"In the basement. I came up by myself."

Troy's lips thinned. "I'm sure. Tell me exactly where they are in the basement."

Erek had to force himself to think rationally. How much could he tell Troy without jeopardizing the others? "Outer hub. I don't know exactly—"

The door clicked open, closed. A man came into view as he stepped around beside Troy. He was blond and slender, with delicate facial features and finely chiseled muscles under a tight-fitting black jumpsuit.

"That'll be all, Murph," Troy said.

The big man turned to look at him. "But Mr. Troy—" Something in Troy's eyes silenced him. He turned quickly and left the room.

The blond man lifted a hand so Erek could see the blackwitch. The 'witch was a finger-thin wand half the length of a man's forearm. The stubby nose concealed a needle, now retracted. The man held it lightly between thumb and forefinger.

"Have you ever felt the 'witch?" Troy asked. "Mr. Burdick is quite accomplished with it. A master, you might say."

The slender man leaned closer, holding the wand an inch from Erek's exposed throat.

"You wouldn't have come here alone," Troy said harshly. "Who came with you?"

Erek was still trying to think of an answer when Burdick lowered the wand. He felt a light touch just below his jaw. He tried to twist away, but the straps held him. He heard the snap of the 'witch an instant before the pain slammed up into his head. He clenched his teeth and released an involuntary grunt. After a moment the pain subsided and left him shuddering in its wake.

"That was the lowest power level," Troy said quietly. "This is one step higher."

Erek felt something at his elbow. *Snap.* Liquid fire shot into his veins, spread across his chest, and raced out to the tips of his fingers. He held his breath and the pain eased slowly. His eyes opened slightly. Above him, Burdick twisted a dial on the handle of the blackwitch.

"Now we've moved it up another notch," Troy said. "Are you ready to tell us the truth?"

With the pain still raging inside his skull, Erek couldn't think clearly. He knew he had to come up with an acceptable answer, but he also knew that he couldn't tell Troy where Joby and Richard were.

He felt his pantleg being rolled up, and the cool tip of the wand on his knee. He pulled desperately against the straps, and had time only to open his mouth before the snap came again. Needles of pain shot up his leg and exploded in his stomach. He arched his back, air hissing between clenched teeth. The wand snapped again. A monstrous bolt of pain lanced straight down through the darkness and exploded behind his eyes . . .

" . . . on the girl, see what she can give us."

Pause.

Erek slitted his eyes. Had he been unconscious?

Troy had turned his back to Erek, and was tightening the straps at the woman's wrists. The man named Burdick had gone around to the other side of the cot. He placed the tip against the woman's arm. She tried to shrink away, but he held the wand firmly in place.

"I'm sorry to put you through this," Troy said in a pleasant voice. "But we have to know what your friend is up to. Would you mind telling me what the two of you discussed there on the flight deck?"

"*She doesn't know anything,*" Erek gritted. "I wanted information, that's all."

Troy ignored him. "Did he mention the others who are with him?"

Erek's mind was racing. What had he told her?

The woman murmured something.

"Excuse me?" Troy leaned closer. "What did you say?"

She spoke again in a low voice. Troy jerked back, color rushing into the scarred tissue of his cheek. He stood rigid, staring down at her. Then he turned to Burdick, his hand out. Burdick gave him the blackwitch without a word. Troy adjusted the handle and the slender, inch-long needle shot out of the end.

"She can't tell you anything!" Erek pulled desperately against the straps that held his wrists.

Burdick looked across at him, his mouth turned up in a thin smile. Troy's eyes did not leave the woman. With quick, sure fingers, he pinched up a fold of flesh on her upper arm and inserted the needle. When the snap came, the woman made a hideous sound and her entire body stiffened.

"*No!*" Erek shouted. "*Stop doing that to her.*"

"Shut up," Troy said calmly. Then, to Burdick: "If he speaks again, kill him."

The wand snapped.

Erek lay still, feeling sick. It suddenly struck home that even telling Troy the truth wouldn't make any difference. Troy wouldn't stop until he'd killed the woman. Then he would come back to Erek.

The snap came again, followed by a thrashing sound from the cot.

A deep coldness began to form inside Erek. It started in the pit of his stomach and moved outward as if it flowed with his blood, chilling it. Along with the coldness came a calm sense of purpose. The woman was here because of Erek. He had to stop Troy and Burdick from killing her. He couldn't do that while he was strapped to the cot. So he had to somehow free himself.

Very simple. One step at a time.

He tested the straps that held his wrists. The one on the left felt as if it might have loosened a little with his earlier struggles. That would be the one to work on. He turned his head slowly to look around. First he had to formulate a plan.

The room was irregularly shaped, roughly ten meters by six. He could guess from the equipment and furnishings that it was a medicenter or first-aid station. The door through which Murph had gone—and as far as Erek could see the only door in the room—was five meters away. A motor hummed nearby; he turned that way and saw that the sound came from a refrigerated storage locker built into the wall.

He moved his eyes back to his left. Both men still had their attention on the woman. Burdick stood on the far side of her and Troy stood between the two cots with his back to Erek. Then Erek saw Troy's sidearm. From the looks of the thick chamber, it was a pellet gun like the one Erek had brought with him. The holster's safety strap hung loose.

Erek's hands twitched. That gun—

Snap. Another cry, hoarse this time as if the woman were growing weaker.

He tested the straps again. They were part of the cot's equipment, probably designed to keep patients in place during the weightlessness of stream skips. They were not meant to keep a determined man prisoner. He put all his strength into leverage at the elbow, concentrating on the strap that had felt loose. It wouldn't give. He fell back, breathing deeply through his mouth.

Snap.

Erek twisted his hand, pushing down with his knuckles against the hard mattress, forcing his wrist up. The strap twisted, and the edge bit viciously into his skin. He gritted his teeth, suppressing a gasp of pain. He felt a rush of warmth and looked down at his arm. Blood welled up over the strap, dark against the white sheet.

Snap!

He forced himself to relax until the pain eased a little, then pulled again. The strap had stretched to its limit.

Then he realized that his hand, slippery with blood, was moving more freely inside the strap. He purposefully moved his hand around in a way that would coat the inside of the strap, then waited.

When the snap came again, followed by the woman's cry of pain, he clenched his teeth and pulled back. His hand slipped free.

He lay still to catch his breath, pressing the wrist against the sheet to staunch the bleeding. Then, careful not to make any sound that might attract Troy and Burdick, he reached slowly across to the strap that still held the other wrist. His fingers were slippery, and the snap from the blackwitch came again before he could unhook the clasp.

Then he had both hands free. Breathing shallowly, he lay back and waited. When Troy bent over the woman again with the blackwitch, Erek lifted himself up on an elbow in one swift motion, twisted sideways, and snatched the sidearm out of Troy's holster. Troy spun around, grabbing for the gun, but it was already firmly in Erek's hand with the safety off. They stared at one another.

"Drop the blackwitch on the floor and get away from her," Erek ordered at last, his voice quivering with strain.

Troy's eyes moved to the bloody hand, then back up to Erek. His face remained expressionless, but when he spoke his voice was heavy with scorn. "You don't have the guts to use that."

Erek punched the firing stud. Burdick jerked sideways as a trail of pellets sprayed the wall behind him. Some of them made little popping sounds as they punched through the thin graymetal. Erek moved the gun back to Troy and made sure Troy could see his thumb on the firing stud.

Troy let the blackwitch fall and stepped over to stand with his back to the wall. Burdick joined him without argument. At Erek's order, he tossed his weapon into a far corner of the room.

Erek reached down to release the straps at his ankles, then threw his legs over the side of the cot. His wrist still oozed blood from the wound just below the heel of the thumb. He pushed himself off the cot and stood, feeling rubbery in the knees. He jerked the gun toward the storage locker. "Inside."

"That's a freezer locker," Troy said.

Erek didn't say anything. Troy stared at him a moment longer, then walked across to the locker, yanked the door open, and stepped inside. Burdick followed with barely a glance at Erek. Erek closed the door behind them and made sure it was latched on the outside. He didn't waste time wondering what their chances were of being found before they froze to death.

He quickly locked the door that led to the outside corridor, jammed the pellet gun into his belt, and began looking for first-aid supplies. He found a gauze pack and a vial of pain-suppressant capsules inside a white cabinet. He swallowed two of the capsules, then tore off a strip of gauze and wrapped it around his wrist, doing a sloppy job with only one hand. Then he returned to the cot where the woman lay.

She was still conscious, although her face was pale. Her eyes followed Erek as he approached. A trickle of blood ran from the wound above her elbow. Another one showed darkly on her neck, just above her uniform collar, and another on a fingertip of her left hand.

Erek's eyes moved to the storage locker. The cold knot hardened inside him.

"Can you move?" he asked after he'd removed the straps from the woman's wrists and ankles.

She drew a ragged breath and tried to pull her elbows under her to sit up.

"Take it easy." Erek placed the first-aid case on the cot and, feeling awkward, put an arm under her shoulders and helped her up, easing her around until she sat on the edge of the cot. He offered the vial. "Take two of these."

It took her a couple of tries to get them down. Then she drew another shuddering breath. "I'll be okay."

Erek opened his mouth to tell her he was sorry for getting her involved in this, then closed it without speaking. Anything he could say would be laughably inadequate. She had told him she would be okay and Erek knew that unless a certain threshold were reached with the blackwitch, its physical effects didn't last too long. The psychological effects were a different story.

"You're bleeding," she murmured.

Erek looked down at his wrist. The makeshift bandage had worked loose and blood ran down his hand. "It'll have to wait—"

"It can't wait. You'll lose too much blood." She reached for the first-aid box, took out the supplies she needed, and laid them on the cot. "Your arm."

Erek looked at the storage locker.

"They aren't going anywhere," she said. "Give me your arm."

He held it out. With surprisingly steady fingers, she began unwrapping the blood-soaked bandage.

Chapter 11

JOBY had never been inside a stateroom before, and hoped fervently that she would never see another one.

At first it was the boredom that bothered her. She tried to overcome that by exploring the room, turning up a few personal items that must have belonged to the former occupants: dirty laundry in the holding chute, holo portraits on the walls, printed commset messages jammed into a two-pronged plastic holder on a low table. Nothing of much interest. An enclosed bathenet occupied one corner of the room; facing it from the other corner stood a small entertainment module with a vidset, a book transcoder, and a computer terminal.

After she and Richard had been waiting half an hour, she began to feel like a trapped animal. Soon after that she was pacing the floor, convinced that the walls were shrinking in on her. The feeling wasn't new to her. She'd complained about it to Gillie once when they had been surprised by a pair of brigs on the fourth level and forced to hide inside a storage cubby for twenty minutes. Gillie told her she had something called closet-phobia.

But it was more than closet-phobia that was bothering her now.

If I don't come back in an hour, go back to the basement, Erek had told her. But the hour had passed ten minutes ago.

She stopped in front of the door. Maybe he had forgotten the room number and was out there in the corridor now, trying to find the right room. He'd told her not to open the door, but . . .

She grasped the handle and slid the door back a few inches. The corridor was dark. She listened for the sound of Erek's footsteps, but heard only silence. She closed the door, turned her back to it, and folded her arms across her chest.

She didn't like the idea of going back to the outer hub without Erek. Not that she felt any particular loyalty to him; if it weren't for Erek and that mouthy guy Blannon, Gillie's message might have gotten through to the Guard. But still, Erek didn't seem like such a bad guy. Kind of wimpy, but he *had* shown some spunk there in the hangar, going after that big lunk even though his hands were tied behind his back. Who knows, he might even have kept the big lunk from frying her or Richard with a carbine blast.

She decided to give him another fifteen minutes.

She wandered over to the end table, picked up one of the chips, and popped it into the 'coder. After listening to a book about Omegan history for several minutes without absorbing a single sentence, she gave up and crossed the room to sit crosslegged on the floor beside Richard. Richard had planted himself in front of the entertainment console when they entered the stateroom, and as far as she knew he had not once taken his eyes from the blank video screen.

She began fidgeting. The digital chronometer above the vidscreen had measured out three minutes since she'd last looked at it. She tapped Richard on the shoulder, got to her feet, and headed toward the door.

"We ain't waiting no more. We're gonna look for him."

Richard stared after her, then unfolded his long legs, pushed himself up, and followed her out of the room.

With Victor Troy's pellet gun ready in his hand, Erek cracked the medicenter door just far enough to peer outside. Stark overhead lighting glared down on a wide corridor. He half expected to find the big man named Murph waiting outside the door. He was relieved to see that the corridor was empty.

He turned back to the woman. "Ready?"

She nodded without speaking. While bandaging his hand, she'd told him her name was Diana Wells. She had been assigned to *Copernicus* fresh out of the UNSA academy on Noura, with a two-year contract as stasis technician. Although she insisted she'd regained most of her strength, her face was still pale and her hands trembled from the effects of the blackwitch. Erek had dropped the vial of capsules into his pocket in case she needed them.

He paused again just outside the door. This part of the ship was obviously a service area, not given to the carpeting and wall holos or other amenities of the residential quarters. The bare walls and floor would carry the sounds of footsteps or voices, but all he heard were the muted mechanical sounds of the ship.

After a few minutes of cautious searching, they found an elevator. When Erek touched the thermal square for the third level, Diana looked at him inquiringly. "I thought we'd be going to the basement. You said your friends were down there."

"Two of them came over with me," he explained. "They're waiting in a stateroom on the third level."

A slight frown crossed her face. "Those children you mentioned? You said they were young—"

"They know their way around. If anyone can get us out of here, they can."

The look on her face told him she had more questions, but the elevator came to a stop before she could ask them. The doors slid open to another wide corridor that looked as deserted as the one they'd just left.

"Have you ever been down here?" he asked as they stepped out.

"A few times." She studied the placard across from the elevator, then tipped her head to the left. "The residential quarters are spinward from here. Once we get close, we should be able to follow the stateroom numbers."

Erek looked down the corridor in the direction she had indicated. Passageways branched off on both sides at regular intervals, with recessed doorways between them. Using this major corridor would expose them to the risk of running into brigs, or possibly even guardsmen. But trying to find a less conspicuous route would take time—something they didn't have.

He tucked the pellet gun into his belt where he could reach it quickly. "Let's go."

They stayed close to the wall, and Erek kept his senses alert. The doors along the corridor were all closed, and the lights down connecting hallways were dim. That made him feel better. The only sounds were their own footfalls on the thin carpet.

They had gone only a short distance when Diana said, "Here it is."

Just ahead a hallway branched to the right. To Erek, it looked exactly like all the others they had passed. Then he realized that the wall placard gave a range of numbers, and the stateroom where he'd left Joby and Richard fell within that range.

His relief at finding it was short-lived. They were still five meters from the hallway when Erek heard a door open behind them and a man's voice:

" . . . cover both sides of sections nine through

eleven. We can split up here and . . . "

Erek pushed Diana into a recessed doorway and tried the handle. Locked. The man behind them was still giving orders. Erek's eyes darted to the opening of the hallway. They would have to make a run for it—

"There they are!" Erek heard the unmistakable click of a weapon's safety release. "Stop right where you are."

Diana pulled Erek's arm. He checked the impulse to run. "Take it easy." If the men were brigs, they were probably trigger-happy. He didn't want to give them an excuse to shoot.

Erek hoped they were guardsmen instead. But when he and Diana turned, they found themselves facing four of Troy's men. The men had already fanned out across the corridor with their weapons drawn.

"Get your hands up and stay where you are," ordered the one in front. His brown fatigues were exactly like those of the others, but his attitude said he was in charge. Erek and Diana complied by lifting their hands as the men advanced slowly down the corridor.

"Mr. Troy wants you back in one piece," said the leader. "Don't do anything stupid."

Erek was jolted by the implications of the statement. He had thought that running into the brigs was bad luck, but nothing more. Had Troy already escaped from the locker and organized a search?

Then he noticed the ship's communicator clipped to the man's belt—and realized he had neglected to take Troy's. Troy had probably called for help the instant the locker door was closed.

A stupid mistake—maybe a fatal one. Whatever thin chance Erek and Diana had for reaching the stateroom had vanished.

The cold knot was back, and it hardened inside Erek as the men drew closer. He couldn't let them take Diana back to Victor Troy; somehow he had made that decision without even thinking about it. Troy could have only one reason for wanting them back alive: so he could continue the questioning. Erek knew that neither of them would survive another session with Troy and his blackwitch.

He waited, tensing the muscles of his legs. He decided to hit the man in the middle first. Maybe he could get his hands on the gun before the others realized what was happening—

Erek heard a sudden sound behind him. Before he could turn, something shot past him moving fast and low, and tumbled across the corridor. He realized it was Joby an instant before she came up flat against the far wall and released her sling. A steel ball hissed through the air and slapped into flesh. One of the brigs yelled and dropped his gun. She fired again. Another man cursed and danced backward, wringing his wrist frantically as if to rid it of a devil. The other two ducked into a doorway farther down the corridor. Erek could see the barrel of a sizzler steading on Joby—

Blam, blam, blam, blam.

He spun around, reaching for the gun in his belt as the explosions crashed down the corridor. Then he saw Richard, crouched at the opening to the hallway from which Joby had come. Smoke drifted from the muzzle of his pistol.

A sizzler beam splashed against the wall beside Erek. He fired a burst of pellets down the corridor, then pulled Diana into the shelter of the hallway. He turned back and looked over Richard's shoulder in time to see Joby flatten herself against the far wall of the corridor, pinned by a barrage of sizzler fire. She released her sling and a steel ball ricocheted down the corridor. Returning sizzler fire snapped against the wall beside her. She looked across at Erek and he could see the knowledge in her eyes: She was running out of time. From their position, the brigs couldn't get a clear shot at her, but Erek knew it would only be a matter of time before one of them reached a better vantage point. If Joby tried to run for the connecting hallway, she would make herself an even better target.

Erek cast a glance back over his shoulder. Behind him, the hallway ran only a few meters to another wide corridor. The stateroom where he had left Joby and Richard must be off that corridor. They had probably been coming this way and heard the brigs.

Erek wondered how long it would take the brigs to realize that some of them could circle around to the other corridor and trap him and the others in a lethal cross fire. He touched Diana on the shoulder and pointed to the adjoining corridor.

"Yell if you see anybody down there."

She nodded and moved a little closer to the intersection. Erek turned back to the outer corridor. Joby still waited for a chance to make her break. Movement caught Erek's eye and his head jerked around as two of the brigs darted across the corridor and dived through another open doorway that was barely five meters away.

Blam, blam, blam.

Spent casings clattered across the deck. Acrid smoke burned Erek's nostrils.

Joby must have realized she had to make her move. When the deafening blasts from Richard's gun came again to drive the brigs behind cover, she bolted from the wall and zigzagged in a long slant across the corridor. She had covered half the distance before she staggered and went down with a stifled cry. She immediately struggled to her feet and took two more faltering steps before her face screwed up with pain and she fell again.

She was still three meters from Erek, and a clear target to the brigs. Before Erek had time to think about it, he'd already flung himself out past Richard, rolled once on the hard metal floor, and came up beside her. He sprayed the corridor with a quick burst of pellets, then jammed the gun in his belt and scooped Joby up in both arms. Richard's gun exploded again and again. Joby clung to Erek's neck as he ran in a weaving path back toward the shelter of the hallway entrance. A loud, sharp *crack* scorched the air over his shoulder and a sizzler beam sparked blue against the wall.

He ran past Richard and continued straight down the connecting hallway with Joby's arms clasped tightly around his neck. Diana waved him on from the other end, then stepped around the corner out of sight.

The boy's gun was still blasting behind Erek when he emerged into the wide corridor and saw Diana holding the doors of an elevator. He angled across the corridor, slowing long enough to look back over his shoulder. Richard ran toward him with the sounds of pursuit close behind. The brigs hadn't waited long to break from cover and take up the chase.

Sizzler fire crackled along the edge of the elevator doors as Erek ran through. Richard stopped and spun around to fire three more shots, driving the brigs back into the hallway. He turned and slipped between the doors just before they came together with a soft thump.

Chapter 12

"THERE has to be an easier way," said Leo Blannon.

Gillie chuckled as he ducked under a steel girder. Then he paused to look up at the massive contraption that squatted over them.

"We're getting close to the motor housing," he said, turning to look up at Blannon. "You okay?"

Blannon didn't answer—he was too busy trying to keep from knocking himself senseless on the steel braces and thick connecting cables that ran every which way. He planned to call for a rest when he caught up with Gillie, but just before he reached him, the boy stepped nimbly over a thick harness of electrical cables and started off again.

They were working their way toward the mechanism that operated one of the solar reflector panels outside the ship. When they first approached it down the aisle that ran between the window strips, Blannon had thought the mechanism resembled a huge, strangely distorted spider. The central housing was a cylinder that rose forty meters from the deck with mechanical growths sticking out all over it. From each side at its approximate midpoint, two massive arms sprouted upward a few degrees off horizontal, then shifted direction at an elbow joint to plunge straight through the deck.

The mechanism clearly fascinated Gillie, and although Blannon wasn't all that interested in expanding his knowledge of solar panel control, the boy had insisted on explaining in detail how it worked. Each arm consisted of three sections that worked together like the booms of a construction crane. The lower boom went through the deck beside the window strip to connect to the solar panel outside the ship. When the motor inside the housing was activated, it would pull or push on the upper sections, which in turn applied force to the lower boom to raise or lower the panel.

According to Gillie, the control system that operated those massive arms had to be somewhere in the central housing. That was what he was after.

Hope it works after all this, Blannon thought. Gillie had given him the bad news there in the basement alcove a few minutes after he had torn into the guts of his commset. The popping sound they had heard came from a program chip inside the microprocessor. Gillie showed Blannon the little metallic gobbets where the chip had melted from the power overload. The commset wouldn't work without the chip, and Gillie had no idea where they could find a replacement.

The boy was bitterly disappointed and blamed himself for the commset's failure even though Blannon tried to convince him that it wasn't his fault.

But facts were facts. Without the commset, they couldn't get through to the Guard post on Semegen IV. Once they'd finally accepted that, they moved on to the next stage of their plan: jamming a solar panel to prevent the skip. That was why he and Gillie had spent the past twenty minutes working their way through this forest of steel braces and thick cables.

Blannon mopped his brow with his sleeve, then hunched down and painstakingly made his way past the brace Gillie had so nimbly ducked under. He reached out to steady himself on another one that angled up toward the housing—and hastily turned loose of the hot metal. The wall that separated the basement from the upper edge of the window strip was only five meters away and Blannon could feel the heat radiating from it. The temperature was at least forty degrees hotter than it had been at the alcove.

"Here we are."

Blannon nearly bumped into Gillie. He took a step back, then realized they had reached the base of the motor housing. Gillie stared straight up the curved side.

"I'll climb up and look around."

Blannon's eyes followed the vertical ladder affixed almost flush to the side of the housing. Ten meters above the floor a service platform with a low railing jutted out from one side. Just below it an identification number was painted in huge white letters: 22 A.

Blannon glanced at his wristwatch. The stream window would open in less than an hour.

"That's a long way up," he said doubtfully.

"Heights don't bother me," Gillie said. He grasped the ladder and began to climb.

Blannon watched him uneasily for a moment. Then he looked around for something to sit on, finally lowering himself heavily onto the narrow ledge that ran around the base of the housing. Heat came up through his slacks. When he glanced up again at Gillie, sweat stung his eyes. He blinked and wiped it away with the back of his arm. He reached for a cheroot and remembered that he'd used the last one before he and Gillie left the alcove.

Damn.

For a moment he sat with his hands hanging limp between his knees. Then, with a deep sigh, he fished the notepad out of his pocket and flipped it open. He spoke a few words and waited for the pad to accept his voice-print. Then:

"Query. Xavier Cassady. Information on subject background prior to joining the Guard."

"Query, reference, Xavier Cassady," the notepad replied. "Broad spectrum search will provide thirty sub-categories on primary sort. Would you like a list?"

"Yes." Then, before it could ask: "Make it verbal."

He leaned back against the hot metal of the housing and closed his eyes as the notepad began naming its database categories that included Xavier Cassady's early childhood, late childhood, education . . .

Blannon let his mind drift with the flow of information. He had become more and more convinced that the leverage Troy had on Cassady was on a personal level. He had heard of instances where families of Guard officers were kidnaped and held hostage in an effort to extract information, or to coerce the officers into doing something for the kidnapers. Maybe Troy had kidnaped somebody close to Cassady and forced Cassady to desert the Guard and hijack *Copernicus*.

"I'll take the one about Family," he said.

The notepad halted its discourse. Then: "Query, reference, specification fault. Abort."

Blannon tried again: "I want the information contained in the subcategory for Xavier Cassady known as Family, Primary."

The pad took a moment to sort through the confusing syntax, then responded: "Parents, Borg Cassady and Annbel Lucas Cassady. Born 29.30 GC on planet Cambridge . . . "

The notepad droned on with details about Cassady's parents, the date they were married, their occupations, religious affiliations. Blannon listened with only half a hope of picking up something new. In truth, he knew it all by heart, including the fact that Cassady's parents still lived on the planet Cambridge. After the hijacking, they had been interviewed and reinterviewed by the news media until they had finally shut themselves away and refused to talk about it.

"No other primary family members still living," the notepad concluded. "Sister Mlissa Lee M'Cmahon died 41.44 GC. Former residence, planet Giant Forest in Sector Tague, Outer Pleiades. One nephew, James Robert M'Cmahon. Do you wish information on Xavier Cassady, secondary family members?"

Something in that last part sounded familiar. Blannon worked his mind around it, couldn't pin it down. Something about Cassady's sister—

"Do you wish information on secondary family members?" the notepad repeated.

"No. Give me—"

A clanking sound from above him drew Blannon's attention. He looked up and saw that Gillie had reached the service platform and was working at something on the side of the housing, just below one of the massive upper arm booms. Blannon opened his mouth to call out to the boy to be careful, but decided that would sound too paternal.

He turned back and shifted his position to ease the crick that was growing in his back. He mopped his streaming brow with the back of his arm.

What was it about Cassady's sister?

"Give me information about Mlissa Lee whatever-her-name-is," he said.

Surprisingly, the notepad knew what he meant. "Son James Robert M'Cmahon born to Mlissa Lee M'Cmahon 36.22 GC on planet Giant Forest in Sector Tague, Outer Pleiades. Mlissa Lee M'Cmahon died 41.44 GC."

Giant Forest. That's what had tickled his memory. Where had he heard that? He sat very still. Then he had it. Something about that reference to Victor Troy's brother. He felt that vague tingling along his spine that told him he was close to something important.

"More," he said.

The notepad responded:

"No other information available, subject Mlissa Lee M'Cmahon."

"What?" he demanded. "There has to be something. What about her birth date?"

"Query, reference—"

"Provide details about birth of Mlissa Lee M'Cmahon."

"No information available."

That didn't make sense. If Cassady's parents lived on Cambridge when his sister was born, her birth should be fully documented. Cambridge was not a backwater planet by any standard.

But Giant Forest was, if it was in the Outer Pleiades. The thought stopped him short. Strange place for Cassady's sister to live, especially if she was born and raised amid the culture and luxury of a planet like Cambridge.

The tingling sensation grew into something more solid.

"Query reference. Travel voucher records, Xavier Cassady, time lag five years."

"Reference, illegal search format."

Blannon pursed his lips, thought it through and tried again. It took him five minutes to coax the notepad into searching the public record of civilian streamer trips over the past five years, with a parallel sort on Xavier Cassady and the planets Cambridge and Giant Forest. When he finally got the answer, he leaned back against the housing and exhaled a long breath.

Then he spoke to the notepad again:

"Query reference, subject Xavier Cassady, sub-category secondary family unit, nephew, James Robert M'Cmahon."

"James Robert M'Cmahon deceased."

Blannon frowned. "Query reference, above subject Cassady. Provide date of death of nephew."

"Reference James Robert M'Cmahon, date of death, 41.44 GC."

That date had a familiar ring. "Query reference. Provide date of death of sister."

"Reference Mlissa Lee M'Cmahon, date of death, 41.44 GC."

Sister and nephew had died on the same date, less than two years ago. "Query, method of death, Cassady's sister."

"Death of Mlissa Lee M'Cmahon due to traumatic penetrative blow to midsection. Pathology consensus: Direct-ray sizzler burst from range of less than four meters."

"Query, method of death, Cassady's nephew."

"Death of James Robert M'Cmahon due to traumatic penetrative blow to neck and upper chest. Pathology consensus: Direct-ray sizzler burst from range of less than two meters."

Blannon gripped the notepad. "Who did it?"

"No individuals sought or apprehended for the unlawful deaths of Mlissa Lee M'Cmahon or James Robert M'Cmahon."

Blannon chewed his lower lip. Maybe there were no official suspects, but . . .

He asked for a parallel sort on the M'Cmahon murders and known criminals. That time he hooked something.

"Parallel reference: Illegal activities on Giant Forest. Common belief expressed by news media: An outlaw group led by fugitives Jock Clyatt and Emil Troy caused two hundred thirty-four civilian deaths, including those of Mlissa Lee M'Cmahon and James Robert M'Cmahon. No legal action taken."

Now he remembered the reference to Giant Forest. That was one of the planets listed by the notepad as having been raided by Jock Clyatt and Emil Troy. The notepad's euphemism for "illegal activities" would have been a raid for merchandise the brigs could sell on the Fringe black market. The fact that no action was taken simply meant that the Guard had been unable to prove they had done it.

The date was right, too. The raid took place just before the Guard yanked the brig operation out from under the Troy brothers and put Emil Troy behind—

Blannon's mouth dropped open. It had been there all along, right under his nose.

"Query," he said to the notepad. "Reference, Jock Clyatt and Emil Troy. Summary data on current whereabouts."

It took the notepad only a moment to find the information and give the answer Blannon expected:

"Jock Clyatt and Emil Troy are presently incarcerated in penal institution, planet Kisatchie."

Chapter 13

DIANA pulled the bandage tight and bound it with an adhesive strip. "How's that?"

In answer, Joby pushed herself out of the chair and hobbled to the door and back. "Feels fine. Let's get out of here before the brigs find us."

The sizzler burn above her knee looked ugly, but apparently hadn't gone through the large muscle of the thigh. The medical spray and tight bandage had taken away the worst of the pain, although Erek had to wonder how long that would last.

"Come on," Joby prompted. "We have to *move*!"

"We'll stay here for now," Erek said.

"How come?" she demanded, swinging around to face him with her hands on her hips. "We should get back to Gillie. Besides, the brigs will be looking for us."

Erek slumped in the room's only armchair, with his head against the backrest and his legs sprawled out in front of him. He felt as if all the energy had flowed out of him. "We're more likely to run into them if we try to make it back to the basement."

"Yeah, but—"

"The Guard will be here before long," he interrupted, too tired to argue. "Then the brigs will be too busy to look for us. We'll go back to the basement then."

"Oh, man." Joby turned away with a sound of disgust.

The elevator they had taken from the third level didn't service the basement. They had been forced to exit on the first level, knowing that the brigs had probably already found a stairway and were on their way down. Diana led them quickly into a residential section where they took refuge in an unlocked stateroom. The brigs knew they were in this area, but there were hundreds of rooms to search. And Cassady and Troy were running out of time.

Erek felt eyes on him and looked up to find Diana watching him. She cleared her throat.

"I'm not sure we can count on the Guard."

Erek frowned.

"I don't think they got your call for help," she went on. "That's why I was surprised when you mentioned it. All the stasis techs are hooked into a message network on the flight deck. We keep track of what's happening in the ship by passing information back and forth."

Erek straightened in the chair. He remembered how quickly Diana had contacted another stasis technician to get information about the upcoming skip sequence. "How would that help you find out about a stream message? You said you don't have access to a commset."

"I said we didn't have any way to send a message," she corrected. "But we can listen in on outbound messages. Cassady's got one of his men stationed over at the CommSec office in the outer hub structure to monitor stream communications in a five-zone block."

So that's what the Guard sergeant was doing over there. "You have a tie-in with that unit?"

She nodded. "We can't transmit, but we can listen to anything that commset unit picks up from outside the local zone. If Semegen IV had gotten a mayday from *Copernicus*, the Guard would be setting up a rescue effort by now. At least they would have called Noura for instructions. But nothing like that has come through."

"Maybe the word didn't get back to you—" But she was already shaking her head.

"After you told me about the call, I used the network to check with Arvid—he's the one keeping tabs on that commset. He hadn't heard anything."

Erek first thought that maybe it had taken longer than Gillie expected to install the interface cable. Then he realized he was grasping at straws. Gillie knew exactly what he had to do with the cable; he would have installed it and had the commset ready for operation hours ago.

Erek hadn't considered the possibility that Gillie didn't send the message. That could mean that the interface cable hadn't worked after all, or that Gillie and Blannon had been picked up by the brigs. The thought chilled him.

His eyes moved down to his wristwatch.

"Thirty minutes," Diana said, still watching him. "That's when the skip window will open. Do you think your friends will be able to get that solar panel jammed?"

"They'll do it," Joby said before Erek could answer. "Gillie can do anything if he sets his mind to it."

"Gillie?" Blannon called. He returned the notepad to his pocket and stepped back a few paces for a better view of what was happening up on the side of the housing. At first he was startled to see that Gillie was no longer working on the service platform. His surprise turned to alarm when he realized the boy had crawled out onto the lower arm boom. In its current position, the boom was inclined at about a twenty-degree angle.

Gillie had climbed up to the shoulder joint and was stretched out flat, working on something at the base of the joint.

"Hey, what're you doing up there?" Blannon called.

The boy's voice drifted down: "I found a service port. I think it'll get me into the control cables."

"Yeah, but . . . " How had he gotten over there? Then Blannon saw the narrow brace that connected the boom to the side of the housing just below the service platform. Gillie must have climbed over the railing and used the brace as a bridge. It couldn't be more than a meter wide. Blannon's eyes measured the distance from the brace to the floor. If his foot had slipped . . .

He shook his head firmly. He wouldn't think about that. "How long will it take?"

After a short pause: "I don't know."

Blannon frowned at his wristwatch, then went back to sit on the ledge at the base of the housing. The skip window would open in less than thirty minutes. During their trek through the basement, Blannon had asked Gillie about the process of putting a ship as big as *Copernicus* through the stream. He wasn't surprised to find out that Gillie knew all about it.

According to Gillie, the drive system had already been making preparations for the skip, and by now would have taken over many of the ship's functions. Fifteen minutes before the skip, the drive system would order the stasis control system to begin slowing the rotation of the two cylinders, and just before that the solar panels would close down.

That was what Gillie was trying to stop. But if the boy's understanding of the events leading up to the skip was right, he had less than ten minutes in which to do it.

At the base of the massive shoulder joint, Gillie was well aware of the time. He'd been working as quickly as he could even while he forced himself to be careful so he wouldn't make mistakes.

At first he'd thought he wouldn't be able to reach a critical control area from the service platform. He had removed one access panel, but all he found were grease fittings. Then he spotted the service port on the lower arm boom and knew instinctively that it was there to provide access to the electronics housing for the main control units in that section.

With barely a glance at the deck ten meters below, he climbed over the railing and stepped briskly across the steel brace to the broader surface of the arm boom, then up the incline to the shoulder joint. A shallow notch had been cut into the top surface of the boom just below the joint. That would be convenient; the notch was the right size for him to crawl into, and it would give him a secure foothold while he worked.

When he reached it, he was surprised to find a large magnetic lock at the bottom of the notch. Feeling a slight premonition, he tipped his head back to look up at the middle boom that towered above him.

What he saw up there sent a chill along his spine.

Blannon leaned back against the housing and looked up at Gillie. If anybody could jam the solar panel, Gillie could. It was remarkable how much the kid knew about machinery. If the theory Blannon had worked out about Xavier Cassady were true, it was especially important that he be prevented from taking *Copernicus* through that next skip window.

Blannon's eyes wandered along the arm boom to the first joint, then down to the point where it descended through the deck. The arm was three times the thickness of a man's body, and looked like a monstrous grasshopper's leg. He remembered what Gillie had told him about how it worked to lower the solar panel. The motor pulled on the first section and that exerted pressure on the second section . . .

Then Blannon realized that the lower boom was too long. It couldn't work the way Gillie had said. He ran his eyes along it again, tracing the movement Gillie had described. Something was wrong. The lower boom would be jammed against the floor before it could move far enough to close the solar panel.

With his curiosity building, Blannon traced the arm again with his eyes. Then he saw it—a second joint halfway up the straight section leading to the shoulder joint where Gillie was working. He remembered that Gillie had said there were three arm booms, not two.

He puzzled over that, then suddenly saw how it worked. As the arm retracted, it would fold over on itself at that joint. By the time the solar panel was flat, the lower section would be . . .

Blannon frowned. That couldn't be right. If it did what he'd worked out in his mind, the third section would fold back on itself right about at the spot where Gillie was working.

"Hey," he called, getting to his feet and stepping back again to bring Gillie into clearer view. "What if you can't stop it? What'll happen if the panel closes while you're still up there?"

Silence.

"Gillie," Blannon called, becoming alarmed.

The thin voice came down: "I've almost got to the cables."

Blannon had been a newsman long enough to know an evasive answer when he heard one. He followed the line of the arm boom again, and the path it would take.

"Maybe you ought to get out of there."

"Can't. I'm not done yet."

"It isn't worth taking the chance. Erek has probably disabled the drive system, anyway."

Gillie remained silent.

Blannon looked down at his wristwatch. Three minutes left.

Gillie lay in the shallow notch with his feet planted firmly against the magnetic lock. His shirt had ridden up and the bare skin of his belly touched the hot metal. He hardly noticed. His tool kit lay open beside him with the handle looped over a large bolt head to keep it from sliding down the inclined boom.

When he'd seen the peg on the boom that soared above him, he knew immediately why it was there. With the arm folded, the peg would fit precisely into the notch and be locked in place with the electromagnet. He couldn't help but feel an appreciation for the simple tongue-and-groove design that added such stability to the mechanism.

It had scared him a little at first. If he were still stretched out in that notch when the arm folded down . . .

But that was silly. Even if he couldn't cut the control link before the solar panel began to close—which he was sure he would—he'd still have plenty of time to squirm out of the notch before the upper boom came down on top of him. The solar panel was big; it would take a long time to close down all the way.

With that reassurance, he got to work.

The access port measured about a meter square, and removing the cover was no more trouble than taking out four butterfly fasteners. Inside, the cables and relays were all neatly coded. That didn't help since he didn't have the service manual to tell him which was which. But Gillie knew about electronics, and he knew which kind of circuit relays were used for computer control and which were used for power supply. He sure didn't want to snip through a power cable. That would fry him for sure, stretched out along the steel boom.

He lay the cover aside, bracing it so it wouldn't slide away, and reached into the opening to begin tracing the control circuits. He worked out the patterns and codes as he went, building up in his mind the network his hands were feeling. Not much different from wiring up those old junkbucket streamers for his uncle back on Joe's Place. Lots of times he'd had to feel his way through a set of connectors stuck in some place that was impossible to get to. Of course, he wasn't as good as Uncle Aaron, not by a long shot. Uncle Aaron was the best—

Enough of that, he chided himself, blinking a sudden sting out of his eye. He had work to do.

Even though he couldn't see them from here, he knew that each of the two arm joints above him had electronics compartments similar to this one, and inside each compartment were motion sensors. That had to be the way it was designed. The main processor in the housing below him worked on a system of constant feedback. As it ordered movement in the arm, the sensors would continually feed arm position back to it while the processor made appropriate adjustments. Gillie also knew that feedback loops were designed to ensure that a single critical failure would shut down the entire unit in order to limit movement that could damage expensive machinery.

Gillie's plan was simple: He would create a critical failure and let the mechanism's own sensors shut it down.

As far as he could tell, the control cables had been installed with triple backup, and each set ran through its own connecting circuitry. That didn't surprise him, but it meant he would have to take precious time to reach all of them. He had already spent fifteen minutes cutting through the primary and secondary circuits, and he was as sure as he could be that he had completely disabled them. He was working his way through a mass of insulation, probing for the tertiary circuit, when Leo Blannon called up to him:

"You've only got one minute!"

Mr. Blannon sounded a little panicky, but Gillie knew he had to stay calm. He stretched his hand farther into the service port, running his fingers along a cable that thickened as it approached the main trunk. He encountered a relay switch and moved past it to the narrower cable beyond. Then he felt the cable's connection at the motor housing. That had to be it.

"Gillie! You have to get out of there . . . "

With his fingertips still touching the cable, he picked up the cutters with his other hand and began to work them into the opening. All he had to do was get the blades over that cable—

Then he heard the low-pitched growl of the big motor starting up inside the housing. He froze. Another sound, a groan, this time from above him. He twisted around and looked up as the boom above him began to move. He stared at the thick tongue of steel coming down, pictured in his mind how it would fit into the notch . . .

He yanked the cutters out of the service port and backed out of the notch as fast as he could. Forget the cable. He had to get out of there before that boom came down and squashed him like a bug. He scrambled to his feet and ran toward the connecting brace that would take him to the service platform. He would be safe there, out of the path of the moving arm—

The arm jerked suddenly, nearly throwing him off as it began to drop. He turned to dash across the brace— and came to an abrupt stop. He had waited too long. The brace wasn't there. In a flash of understanding, he knew why. The brace had been latched into place to stabilize the arm against the Coriolis force while the arm was extended and the cylinder turning. With the first movement of the lower boom, the brace had automatically released and folded down out of the way.

He had no way to get back to the service platform, and it was ten meters to the deck below.

"Gillie!"

He slipped and went down on one knee as the angle of the boom steepened. Then he turned and scrambled back along the boom to the access port. He flung himself into the opening notch, barely hooking a hand over the lip of the opening before the angle became so steep that he would have started sliding back. He thrust his

other hand into the electronics housing and began probing frantically with the cutters. The motor hummed,
sending vibrations through the housing.

"*Gillie . . .*"

His toolbox pulled loose and slid past him, followed
by the port cover. Several seconds later he heard them
crash far below, the tools scattering. With a jolt, the
lower boom reached the bottom of its arc and started
back up, gaining momentum. He didn't have to look up
to know that the boom above him was bending now at
the joint to swing down to meet the lower one.

Desperately, he lay the cutters aside and used his
fingers to feel for the cable. There it was, right where
he'd expected to find it. He fixed the location in his
mind, snatched up the cutters, and once again fished for
the cable. Something sharp snagged his hand, tearing
skin. The boom pivoted closer, groaning as its massive
weight shifted. He squirmed sideways, pressing himself
against the hard steel. The cutters closed over something
and relief surged through him. He clenched his hand. A
cable snapped, but the boom kept moving. He had cut
the wrong cable.

He lunged again, and felt another cable slip between
the blades of the cutters. A thought crossed his mind: *If
this isn't the right one, will my body be enough to jam
the solar panel?*

The tongue of steel came down against him as his
hand grasped convulsively at the handle of the cutters . . .

Victor Troy leaned back in the captain's chair, watching the numbers as they flashed across the countdown
screen in front of him. The stream window would open
in fifteen minutes, but preparations for the skip were
already being made throughout the ship.

"Looks good," said Klaus Burdick, standing beside
him.

Troy scanned the monitors that were part of the command module. He was suddenly aware that his teeth were clenched together. He parted them with an effort.

It's going to work.

Why did he have to keep telling himself that? The stasis and k-stream drive systems had been tested less than an hour ago. The environmental control system was still shaky, but according to Burdick that wasn't crucial to the skip.

After two years of running from the Guard, hiding out in the worst imaginable dungheaps of Fringe planets, he would have the resources to make a fresh start. And, he thought with a grim smile, he would get in a few kicks at the Guard at the same time. He was long past due settling that score.

The timer passed the fourteen-minute mark.

The desk communicator buzzed. He whirled around and snatched up the handset.

"Yes? What is it?"

"Everything's going as planned on this end," said Xavier Cassady. "How's it look up there?"

Troy made a conscious effort to get a grip on his jangling nerves.

"No problems," he answered. As if Cassady didn't know. Cassady had decided to remain in his office during the skip, but Troy had no doubt that he was following the countdown on his own monitors.

"I'll come down immediately after we've reached the focal point. We'll contact Kisatchie then." Cassady paused before going on. "I've gotten word that twenty of your men have gathered in the hangar, near the *Wasp*. Mind telling me what they're doing there?"

"Waiting," Troy answered. "They want to be ready to move the instant we give the order."

"That order won't be given until after we've made contact with penal officials."

"I know that."

Another brief pause.

"I hope you remember our agreement," Cassady said

heavily. "All aspects of it."

"Of course, Colonel. I'll see you later, then?" He clicked off before Cassady could reply.

Klaus Burdick chuckled. "I hope you remember our agreement," he mocked.

Troy's hand went to the communicator strapped to his belt. After the skip, he would use that to give his own orders to his men in the hangar. Unlike Burdick, he knew better than to underestimate Cassady. As far as he could tell, Cassady had done nothing to protect the *Wasp* even though he had to know Troy would try to grab it.

Troy felt the ache in his jaw again and realized he'd clamped his teeth together once more. He settled back into the captain's chair. *Relax. Nothing can go wrong now—*

"Stasis malfunction, upper quadrant four, starboard."

Troy jerked straight up in the chair and slammed his palm against the deskset override to open an emergency channel.

"Repeat that," he barked.

"We have a fault condition with solar panel controls in upper quadrant four, starboard," the stasis tech said.

"*Fault condition?*" Troy snapped. "What does that mean?"

"One of the solar panels won't close. We'll have to abort the skip."

Troy's eyes shot to the countdown screen. Ten minutes. He spun around to Burdick. "What's he saying? What's happening?"

Burdick leaned over the console to study the lower readout screen. "Can't tell from here." He turned to look at the reference number that glowed beside the commset and pointed out the corresponding number stenciled above a work station on the third tier. "Maybe we can find out—"

Troy shouted into the commset: "Don't do anything until I get there."

"But the drive system will . . . "

The rest of the words were lost as Troy yelled at Burdick to follow, bolted from the chair, and ran toward the escalator. They took the steps two at a time to the third tier and went around the perimeter at a full run. The stasis technician was punching at his console keyboard when they arrived.

"What are you doing?" Troy demanded.

The man typed another command. The readout screen in front of him rippled with rows of changing numbers.

"*I said what are you doing?*" Troy screamed.

"The trouble's been verified from two other stations," the technician replied, unruffled by Troy's outburst. "I'm trying to find out what's causing it."

"Can you fix it?"

"Give me a minute and I'll tell you."

Troy's eyes darted to the countdown numbers pulsing in the corner of the readout screen. "We don't *have* a minute."

The man remained silent. Troy stood seething beside him while information flowed across the readout screen. A moment later the man shook his head and leaned back in his chair.

"It's a mechanical breakdown. We'll have to send somebody down to take a look."

Troy stared at him. "It *can't* be a mechanical breakdown. Everything checked out less than an hour ago."

"Something's happened since then—"

"*Your* people checked everything out."

"One of the solar panels won't lock." The man seemed not to notice Troy's threatening tone. He frowned at the information on the readout screen. "Odd. It's almost as if something's been jammed under the panel itself. Or maybe there's a breakdown in the structural hardware." He swiveled around and looked up at Troy with eyes that were maddeningly calm. He was older than Troy, with graying hair and a thick mustache. "Those are facts. Nothing we can do to change them."

Troy spun around to Burdick. "Get down there with some technicians and fix it. We have to get through that window—"

The stasis console beeped. Troy turned around in time to see a flood of new information roll across the readout screen.

"Too late," said the man. "The drive system aborted the skip. We'll have to try for the next window."

Sudden rage filled Troy. He gripped the material of the man's shirt below his neck and forcibly yanked him out of the chair. The man outweighed Troy, but the adrenaline charging through Troy's veins more than made up the difference. Troy's sizzler was in his hand, the muzzle digging into the man's ribs. The man stiffened, his eyes widening.

"Now just a minute—"

His words were cut off as the sizzler snapped. The technician grunted and jerked back against the work station. Burdick stepped out of the way as the body fell heavily to the floor.

Troy holstered his sizzler, the fury inside him giving way to a hard but controllable anger. Activity around them ceased and the flight deck went suddenly still.

"When will the next window open?" Troy asked.

Burdick consulted the stasis readout screen. "A little over two hours."

"Are Murph and the others still looking for those kids in the basement?"

Burdick shook his head. The sudden violence and the dead man at his feet didn't faze him. He'd worked with Victor Troy long enough to know that was how Troy dealt with the fury when it raged inside him. And when he was around Troy, Burdick never let his hand stray far from his gun. "They all went back to the hangar. That's where you wanted them."

Of course. How could he have forgotten?

"Those kids did something to the solar panel," Troy said, calming himself. "Get some men down there to look for them. Make sure they check out the area where the panel jammed. Any word on the search for that streamer pilot and the black girl?"

"No . . ."

"Have the basement ports been sealed off?"

"Not all of them. We don't have enough men to do that."

Troy went on as if he hadn't heard:

"Make sure all the rooms in that first-level unit are searched. They have to be down there. When they're found, kill them. Don't bother bringing them back, just kill them. That includes the kids."

"We'll have to pull everyone out of the hangar . . ."

"Do it, do it," Troy said, waving his hand. "I'll be in my office."

Burdick stared at him, then touched his index and second finger to his forehead in a sort of half salute and turned away.

Troy's head was splitting by the time he reached his office. He took two of the red pills, and had barely settled in the chair behind his desk when his handset buzzed. He swiveled around and picked it up.

"Lieutenant Hollins, Mr. Troy. Colonel Cassady would like to see you in his office immediately."

Troy thought about telling Hollins exactly what Cassady could do with his urgent summons. But he knew he couldn't. If they were going to have to wait for that next window, he would need Cassady and his men a few more hours.

After that . . .

Troy gritted his teeth. "Tell him I'm on my way."

Chapter 14

"GILLIE?"

Silence.

"*Gillie!*"

Leo Blannon stared up at the steel arm high above him. The two lower booms had folded together completely. The third boom was almost vertical, as it would be with the solar panel flat against the hull.

And Gillie was still there between the two lower booms. At the last moment, when the middle section of the arm came down, Blannon thought he'd heard something—a crunching sound? Or was it part of the huge mechanism—?

Suddenly, with a spurt of energy he wouldn't have believed possible, he jumped for the ladder and began climbing hand over hand up the side of the housing. He pulled himself over the railing of the service platform and took three long strides to the connecting brace. He had seen the brace fold down earlier, but now, with the arm stationary, the brace had again latched into place.

He stepped gingerly over the railing and eased himself out along the brace. When he reached the lower boom, he was close enough to see the edge of the notch in which Gillie had been working and the steel peg on the upper section that fit down into it. He could also see that the boom hadn't quite come down all the way. The steel peg had not gone fully into the notch.

Cold horror gripped him as he realized why the boom had stopped. Gillie's body was crushed under all that steel. Blannon swallowed. He had seen blood and death many times in his years as a newsman, but never anything this . . . close to him—

"Mr. Blannon, are you there?"

Blannon sagged, nearly lost his footing, and grabbed for the arm boom. He tried to speak, coughed dry air instead.

"Mr. Blannon?"

Blannon tried again: "Gillie? Are . . . are you all right, boy?"

"Sure. I'm tying off these wires. Don't want them to short together and start up that motor again."

Blannon looked at the massive boom beside him. *No*, he thought giddily, *we sure don't want that to happen*.

He stood motionless, sucking in great gulps of air. A moment later a leg appeared between the two booms, then another one. Then Gillie crawled out through the lower edge of the notch, working his way carefully around the steel peg.

"Can you give me a hand, Mr. Blannon?"

Blannon edged closer, suddenly conscious of the sheer drop to the graymetal deck below. Gripping the boom for support, he held out his hand. Gillie grasped it and swung out around the peg. He looked out over the edge of the boom, sucking the back of a skinned hand.

"Jeez. Probably never will find all my tools down there." He stepped past Blannon and crossed the connecting brace to the service platform. He stopped at the railing and turned back. "Coming, Mr. Blannon?"

Blannon had not moved. *Did I really come out across that narrow brace? God, it's hardly wide enough for my feet* . . . A rod of tension grew along his spine as he realized he would have to let go of the boom to get back across to the service platform. He'd never considered himself acrophobic, but he'd never had to walk across a narrow beam ten meters above the floor. You didn't need acrophobia to feel uneasy about that.

As he stood there trying to work up the courage to take a step, he heard a sound from somewhere below. Then a male voice drifted up. Gillie heard it, too.

"Mr. Blannon," he whispered urgently. "Come on. They might see you out there."

Blannon was frozen in place with his feet planted firmly and a death grip on the arm boom. The voices came again, closer this time:

"Waste of time, if you ask me. No way those kids could've done anything down here."

"Yeah, but we gotta check it out. Orders is orders."

Blannon caught a glimpse of them through a tangle of braces and cables: two men in brown fatigues walking side by side along the aisle that led between the window strips.

"Here it is," one of them said. His arm lifted and he seemed to be pointing directly at Blannon. "Number twenty-two A." They passed out of Blannon's view. "Looks like it's closed down to me."

Silence for a few minutes. When the voices came again, the men had moved to a point directly under Blannon.

"Think we ought to go up and take a look?"

Pause. Blannon's heart hammered; sweat stung his eyes. He dared not move.

"Naw. Too hot to be climbing around on all that steel. Probably a computer foul-up. They'll have to send some of those techs down to fix it. I told 'em that to start with."

The other man didn't offer any argument. The sound

of their footsteps receded and a moment later Blannon saw them retracing their way down the aisle.

Gillie waited until the sounds had long faded, then said: "Mr. Blannon?"

Blannon drew a deep breath. With his eyes straight ahead, he began moving slowly out along the brace, keeping a tight grip on the arm boom. When he ran out of solid metal to hold onto, he was still three meters from the railing. He lifted his eyes to Gillie.

The boy must have seen some of the panic in them.

"I'll help you, Mr. Blannon." He climbed effortlessly over the railing, stepped out across the connecting brace, and took Blannon's hand. "We'll go real slow."

Somehow the grip of Gillie's small hand helped. It gave Blannon a sense of security, even though the logic centers in his brain kept telling him that if he slipped there was no way the boy could keep him from falling. Together they made it to the service platform. Blannon clung to the railing, drawing air in great ragged gulps. Then he eased himself over and collapsed onto the platform with his back against the housing.

"They won't be back for a while," he managed, still fighting for air. "I have to rest."

Gillie squatted beside him. "At least we stopped that solar panel. Colonel Cassady won't be able to skip until they fix it."

The boy was right. With all that had happened, Blannon had forgotten all about their reason for coming up here in the first place. The window had already passed, and Blannon knew the ship hadn't skipped. The drive system hadn't even gotten far enough in the program to stop the cylinder rotation.

"Ready to start down?" Gillie asked.

"In a minute." Blannon sucked in another deep breath, letting it out slowly. He didn't relish the thought of going back down that vertical ladder. He leaned his head back against hard metal. "I've been wanting to ask you something."

Gillie waited, his eyes suddenly wary.

"Are you really Joby's brother?"

Gillie's eyes widened in surprise. Blannon wondered briefly what kind of question he had expected.

"Not exactly," Gillie answered.

"What did she mean, then?"

"We grew up together, that's all."

"With Richard, too?"

Gillie nodded.

"Do you and Joby have something personal against Troy?"

Gillie's eyes dropped to his clasped hands. "What makes you think so?"

Blannon hunched his shoulders slightly. "The way you use his name, like it's a dirty word. Does it have anything to do with what happened to your uncle?"

Gillie was silent a moment. Then: "Troy killed him."

Blannon waited while Gillie fought with something inside. Finally the boy spoke again. "We're from Joe's Place."

Blannon frowned. He'd heard of a planet—"In the Malachi Bloc?"

Gillie nodded, his eyes still lowered. Blannon had once done a feature story about the Malachi Bloc, a string of Fringe planets in a far upstream corner of Omega. It had started out as a political entity—a half dozen planets bound together in a single stream zone by a trade agreement. The agreement fell apart for the usual reason—greed—along with the social structure of the planets. The Guard troops were spread thin that far out, and over time the Malachi Bloc became a haven for outlaws and misfits and other dregs of society. Many of the larger brig bands used Malachi planets as their bases of operations.

"You grew up there?" Blannon asked.

Gillie nodded. "All three of us."

"With your Uncle Aaron?"

Gillie didn't answer for a long moment. He averted

his face and Blannon was sorry he'd brought up the subject. He suggested they drop it, but by then Gillie wanted to talk.

"My grandpa settled on Joe's Place back when the planet wasn't too bad, before the brigs moved in. Uncle Aaron and my dad were born there. Grandfather died before I was born and my dad died when I was little. So I lived with Uncle Aaron." Gillie kicked his toe against a railing post, spent a moment looking out at the basement. Blannon kept silent.

"Uncle Aaron ran a streamer repair shop in a town called Bly Harbor. He was the best streamer mechanic in Malachi." Gillie's voice cracked. He cleared his throat and went on. "He had magic fingers and a real passion for anything mechanical. Even if he'd never seen a piece of machinery before, he could spend ten minutes with it and show you how it worked."

"I'd say you inherited some of that," Blannon observed.

That brought a flush to the boy's cheeks and a quick, self-conscious grin. "Uncle Aaron taught me. He always said I should be an engineer, not a mechanic." The grin faded. "Uncle Aaron wanted to get away from Joe's Place. Soon as he could scrape together enough money, we were going. All four of us. That was his dream."

"Why did Joby and Richard live with you?"

"They were street kids. They started hanging around Uncle Aaron's shop because he gave them food. Eventually he took them in."

"What about their parents?"

"Dead, probably. Joby doesn't know for sure; Richard took care of her from the time she can remember. He might know how it all came about, but there's no way to find out from him."

"Street kids," Blannon mused. "That explains Joby's skill with the sling."

Gillie nodded. "When you're a kid on your own in

Bly Harbor, you either learn to take care of yourself or you don't grow up."

A long silence drew out. Blannon knew they would have to get moving before long.

"How did your uncle get involved with Victor Troy?" he asked.

The boy's face darkened and for a moment Blannon thought he wouldn't answer. When he spoke at last, his voice had gone harsh and bitter. "Troy came to Joe's Place a couple of years ago. He lived there; not in Bly Harbor, but in a town not far away."

"Hiding from the Guard," Blannon said. "That would have been after the Guard broke up his organization and sent his brother to Kisatchie."

Gillie shrugged. "I s'pose. A few weeks ago, Troy brought his ship to Bly Harbor with a blown stator motor. Somebody had told him Uncle Aaron could fix it. After he did, Troy killed him."

Blannon frowned. "Why?"

"Troy was probably making plans to skip to *Copernicus*. Uncle Aaron must have seen something that tipped him off. Maybe he overheard Troy talking about it to one of his men. Troy wouldn't want to take a chance that Uncle Aaron could get word to the Guard about it."

"Plausible enough," Blannon said. "But how did you and the others get aboard *Copernicus*?"

"That wasn't supposed to happen. My fault. Joby wanted to kill Troy for what he'd done, but I had another idea. I wanted to sabotage his ship so it would break down at the end of the first skip sequence. Troy would be stranded out in space. Then I could call the Guard and tell them where to pick him up." He paused. "Uncle Aaron didn't like violence. That's how he would have done it."

"What happened?"

"We sneaked aboard his ship to rig up a delayed charge in the drive processor. Troy fired up the engines and took off before we could get out. He came straight to *Copernicus*. We slipped out after he'd docked and hid in the basement.''

"Cassady had already hijacked the ship?"

Gillie nodded.

"Quite a story." Blannon wondered if he would ever get a chance to write it. He had more questions, but when he checked his wristwatch, he decided they would have to wait. He and Gillie had already stretched their luck by staying here this long.

Getting down the vertical ladder was even more difficult than Blannon had expected. He rested again at the bottom while Gillie gathered the tools he could find and replaced them in his tool kit, and they spent the next half hour making their way back through the basement to the alcove.

Blannon expected to find Erek and the others waiting for them. They should have returned long ago, but he could see no sign they had ever been back.

"They must have run into trouble." He sat down on a graymetal crate and accepted a tin of warm fruit juice Gillie had found in a storage crate. "We'll have to go over and find out what happened."

"To the other end of the cylinder?" Gillie looked doubtful. "They could be anywhere over there. Do you think we can find them?"

"Probably not by ourselves," Blannon admitted. "But we might be able to get some help."

Gillie's face registered surprise. "From who?"

"Xavier Cassady."

Erek leaned back in the armchair and closed his eyes, feeling relief as much as anything else. The skip window had passed, which meant that Gillie had accomplished what he'd set out to do. That was a relief in another way—it meant Leo and Gillie hadn't been caught after all.

But according to Diana, another window would open

in less than two hours. Erek knew that Cassady and Troy wouldn't let a jammed solar panel stop them a second time.

"We have to get a message to the Guard," he said slowly, his eyes still closed. "That's our only real hope. We have to find an interstream commset."

"All the 'sets in the flight deck have been disabled," Diana said. She sat on the small couch across from him. "As far as I know there's only one still working in this end of the cylinder. That's in Cassady's office."

"Let's go," Joby said. "Anybody gives us trouble" —she pointed a finger and made a zapping sound— "we'll fry 'em."

Erek's heart was with Joby; he felt an almost overwhelming need to do *something* to strike back at Cassady and Troy. That cold knot inside him demanded action. But at the same time he didn't like the idea of trying to get into Cassady's office by force. Something Diana had said earlier came back to him. "You mentioned an emergency command center. Where is it?"

"On the twentieth level, out near the hub."

"Wouldn't that be equipped with an interstream commset?"

She considered. "You're right. But somebody's bound to be guarding it."

"Maybe not. Cassady won't expect us to go up there." Then he had another idea. "What would we have to do to get into the ship's drive system from there?"

She started to say something, stopped, frowned. "I don't think the emergency command center will help. It can only be activated by codes, and only Captain M'Hing and a few of his top officers would have them. None of them are still on the ship."

"The commset, too? It wouldn't be operable?"

She shook her head. Then she became thoughtful. "Unless . . ."

"Unless what?" Erek prompted when she lapsed into silence.

"Well, the main reason for the emergency command center is to give backup control and communication links in case of a major problem on the flight deck. If there were a disaster on the flight deck, drive and stasis control would shift automatically to the ECC. I'm sure the commset would be activated, too."

"What kind of disaster?"

She thought about it. "Fire. Major computer malfunction. Anything bad enough to shut down the control system."

"Then Cassady wouldn't be able to complete the skip?"

She shook her head. "Not from the flight deck. Drive system control would shift to the ECC."

Erek's eyes moved to Joby and Richard, then back to Diana. "The brigs are probably watching the main entrances to the flight deck. Are there any other doors they may have missed?"

She thought about it and nodded. "A few service entrances, probably. They aren't too thorough."

He turned to Joby. "Do you think you can get into the flight deck?"

"Sure. Just tell us how to get there."

"What about your leg?"

She slapped the bandage. "No problem."

He hoped she was right. "That's what we have to do, then."

Diana had a puzzled look on her face. "*What's* what we have to do?"

"Create a disaster on the flight deck," he told her. "If Joby and Richard can do that, you and I will have to be ready to take over when control of the ship passes to the emergency command center."

Chapter 15

JOBY and Richard emerged from the service stairway and found the passageway that opened out to the third tier of the flight deck. The brigs were stationed at the main entrances on each tier, but hadn't bothered with the service doors. That was typical of their way of thinking; they expected anyone trying to get into the flight deck to shoot their way through because that was the way they would've done it.

The work stations close to this service door weren't occupied, and Joby and Richard ducked behind one without being seen. Joby's leg was throbbing from the long climb up the stairway, but she thought it would hold out long enough to get the job done. It would have to.

A glance between the console and the desk unit gave her the general layout: the big, oval-shaped command module on the lower level, the moving escalators, the wall placards that marked stairway entrances on each tier, the location of the washrooms and offices. A group of brigs hung around the command module. Joby heard faint voices, followed by a staccato burst of laughter.

Black and gray uniforms were scattered throughout the flight deck, although most of them were on the two lower tiers. The technicians worked silently at their console units and, except for the muted voices of the brigs, the only sounds in the room were faint beeps and blips from the work stations and an occasional buzzing sound that Joby thought came from those machines that made the little plastic data chips.

Joby's eyes were good; even from this distance she could see the black facing plate on the command console below the readout screen. Diana had first thought they would have to destroy the entire command module, somehow start a fire or blow it up. Then she remembered the switching processor inside the main console that she had learned about in a school she'd gone to. If they could break through the plate and damage the processor, she thought it would be enough to knock out the command module and shift control of the ship to that other room upstairs.

But Joby saw right away that damaging the processor wouldn't be easy. The black plate was only a little bigger than her hand. According to Diana, the plate was heavy plastic, like the rest of the console unit. Richard's pistol would be able to blast through it, but the handgun was a short-range weapon—too risky with a target so small from this far away. Joby knew she could hit the plate with her sling, but she wasn't as sure that a steel ball would break through it. With all those brigs down there, she knew that she and Richard would only get one chance.

Which meant they would have to get closer to the command module before making their move.

Her eyes moved around the flight deck again. The closest escalator was ninety degrees around the perimeter. The brigs at the command module wouldn't have a clear view of it unless they got up and turned around to look and, from the way they were flapping their jaws at one another, she didn't think there was much chance of that.

She and Richard could take that escalator to the second tier and work their way around to a spot directly above the command module. From there, Richard could use his gun to put a few slugs into the black plate, then they would have to run back up the escalator to the third tier and around it to the service door.

She measured it out, then reluctantly shook her head. Too far, especially with her bum leg. They would never make it back to the door before the brigs started shooting. She knew they wouldn't hesitate to shoot her and Richard in the back, just like they had murdered Uncle Aaron.

Another idea surfaced. She dismissed it at first; even the brigs wouldn't be stupid enough to fall for that. Then she took another look at them and changed her mind. Her eyes went to the two who were leaning against the wall near the main entrance on the second tier. Her lips turned up in a slow grin. This could be fun.

First she would have to scout the territory.

She gave Richard a palm-down sign to stay put. Then, still crouching, she edged back out through the service door. Diana had mentioned another entrance near the back of the lower tier . . .

A few minutes later she was back, still grinning. This would work even better than she'd hoped. She checked the wristwatch Diana had given her. They had synchronized the time of the hit and she still had five minutes left. Plenty of time.

She used her hands to explain her plan to Richard. Then, while Richard checked his pistol to make sure it was fully loaded, she took a few steel balls from her pouch and put them in her mouth where they would be in handy reach.

Keeping their heads below the level of the railing, they started around the perimeter toward the escalator. A stasis tech looked up from her work as they approached. Surprise registered, and Joby gave her a big grin with an index finger to her lips. The technician stared at them as they went by, but remained silent. They passed several others, but all of them had the presence of mind to keep silent.

They rode down the escalator on their heels, keeping their heads down, stepped off on the second tier, and moved down the aisle to take cover behind an unoccupied work station. Joby edged forward to peer out over the railing. The two brigs at the second-level entrance stood directly across from her.

She turned back to Richard with her hand out, palm down. Then she began to work her way toward the two men. She moved silently on the balls of her feet, darting from work station to work station when she was sure the men were looking the other way. At the same time she made sure that she didn't expose herself to the group down at the command module. The stasis techs kept their eyes fixed steadily on their readout screens while she went past and two of them even shifted their position slightly to help block her from the view of the brigs.

It took most of the five minutes to reach an empty work station from which she could get a clear view of the two men near the entrance. She raised herself up far enough to look out across the railing to the other side of the tier. She couldn't see Richard, but she knew he was there.

Then she turned back to the men, lifted her sling, and took careful aim. A steel ball whistled through the air and bounced off the skull of the man closest to her.

The results were even more spectacular than Joby had hoped. The man grunted and took a step backward, caught the back of his legs on the railing, and toppled over with his arms flailing. He had time to yell once before he crashed into an empty work station on the lower level. Joby used the sling again and hit the other man between the eyes while he was still fumbling for his sidearm. He dropped his gun and staggered backward, clawing at his face. He would be out of commission for a while.

A shout came from below. The brigs down at the command module had spotted her and were rushing toward the escalator. She grinned with satisfaction when she saw that none of them stayed behind at the command module. She had been right in her earlier estimation: They weren't too bright.

She waited until they reached the escalator and started up, then she turned and ran back around the aisle. The men shouted at her to stop and one of them managed to get off a sizzler beam that splattered bright blue against the railing beside her.

She ducked down an intersecting aisle that she knew from her earlier scouting mission would take her to an outer corridor. She raced up to the sliding door, hit the wall plate, slipped through the instant the door opened wide enough, and palmed the plate on the opposite side to close it. Another sizzler beam came through the opening and sliced the air beside her right shoulder. By the time the door slid shut, she was already halfway down the corridor to the waiting elevator. She thrust her arm inside to punch one of the buttons near the top of the control panel and yanked it out again as the doors began to slide together.

She ran back to the service door and flung herself behind a stack of flattened storage boxes an instant before the door whispered open and the brigs rushed through. They stood in a confused knot, tripping over each other as they voiced conflicting ideas about which way to go. Apparently it didn't occur to them to split up so they could cover more area. Joby had to clamp her lips to keep from laughing out loud.

Then one of them shouted and pointed at the indicator lights above the elevator. They rushed toward it in a great ungainly group, then veered toward the stairwell a few meters farther down the corridor.

When the door closed behind them, Joby got up from her crouching position, wincing as a sharp pain lanced through her leg. *Don't give up on me now.* Limping, she went back through the sliding door into the flight deck. A nearby stasis technician turned when he heard the door slide shut. He grinned and gave her a thumbs-up.

Joby grinned back, feeling good despite the pain in her leg.

From the railing she could see Richard already on his way down the escalator, taking the slow-moving steps two at a time. He turned to look up at her as he reached the command module. She checked Diana's wristwatch. Thirty seconds left. Close enough. She looked back down at Richard and drew a finger slowly across her throat.

Richard turned back to the control console and fired six shots directly into the black plate. A woman screamed and a babble of voices broke out. With the shots still echoing around the flight deck, Richard turned and ran back up the escalator. Blue smoke from his pistol drifted toward the ceiling, drawn into swirling eddies by the ventilating system.

Getting up to the twentieth level was easier than Erek expected. Diana had been up here only once—during her initiation tour of the ship. But she knew her way around, and led the way from the first-level stateroom down a series of narrow passages to a freight elevator that serviced the outer wall of the hub structure. They took that elevator to the twentieth level, then followed the main corridor to another side passage that branched away to the ECC.

Twice while they were in the main corridor they had to duck out of sight to let noisy groups of brigs pass. Both times Erek was surprised at how steady he remained. He wondered: *Am I getting used to this?*

He was glad to see that only one brig stood guard outside the door of the ECC, leaning against the wall with his carbine slung loosely over his shoulder. He looked as if he were wilting from boredom as much as from the stifling heat. Erek and Diana watched him from a recessed doorway several meters away. Erek had the pellet gun and Diana carried one of the sizzlers from Joby's pouch. Erek had already made sure she knew how to use it.

When his wristwatch showed that less than a minute remained before the time they had agreed on with Joby, Erek checked the corridor again. Still empty, except for the single brig. He signaled Diana and they stepped out of the doorway with their weapons leveled. A ceiling fan hummed directly above the brig and he didn't notice them until Erek spoke:

"Put your hands up."

The man whirled around, reaching for his gun.

"Don't!" Erek said sharply.

The man stiffened. He was young, Erek realized— barely older than Richard. When he saw the pellet gun and the sizzler, he licked his lips and moved his hands away from his gun.

"We want inside that room," Erek said, working to keep his voice firm. "Don't touch the carbine. Lower it to the floor with the strap and put your hands together on top of your head."

The man didn't argue. His eyes remained on the pellet gun. Even though he was young, he had probably been in the company of Victor Troy long enough to know that a pellet gun could rip a man apart in less than a second. At Erek's order, he stepped back against the far wall with his hands still clasped. Erek reached down to retrieve the carbine and handed it across to Diana. While she held it on the brig, Erek wrenched the dogs and opened the door to the ECC. As he had expected, the door was a sealing lock, designed to prevent loss of air from the ECC in case of a major hull puncture or other disaster in the ship.

He briefly considered ordering the man inside, then

decided against it. Troy would know that control had shifted to the ECC long before the man could report it to him.

After he and Diana were inside, he pushed the door shut and twisted the dogs to secure it. Then he turned to look over the room. It was a smaller version of the flight deck with the work stations—Erek estimated there were less than half the number that were on the flight deck —arranged in two concentric rings around the command module. The module was at a lower level than the rest of the room, surrounded by a low security wall. From the single entrance, a few steps led down to a control area consisting of three readout screens facing a swivel chair, a computer console, and a full-service commset.

As he and Diana approached the module, Erek saw a message blinking on the central readout screen:

DRIVE CONTROL INTERRUPT MAIN MODULE
AWAITING INSTRUCTIONS . . .

"They did it," Diana said incredulously. Then she turned to Erek with wide eyes. "We have control of the ship."

They had control now, but Erek wondered how long they would keep it. They were committed—trapped in this room with one pellet gun, a long-barreled carbine, and a nearly discharged sizzler. By now, Cassady and Troy probably knew that control had shifted to the ECC.

Erek's eyes returned to the sealing door. In a few minutes thirty-five brigs and more than a dozen well-armed guardsmen would be trying to break through it.

Chapter 16

GILLIE closed the door and turned to look up at the wall placard. He and Blannon stood in a narrow, low-ceilinged corridor in the cylinder's sunward hub structure.

"There's a stairway this way," Gillie said, hooking a thumb to his left. "That'll take us to the fourth level."

Blannon kept silent as he peered doubtfully in the direction the boy indicated. He didn't look forward to climbing three flights of stairs.

"Colonel Cassady's office is in the navigation section—spinward, about ninety degrees," Gillie went on. "You still think we should try to reach him?"

"We have to," Blannon answered. During the long trek through the basement he had told Gillie about the information he had gotten from the notepad, and why he thought they could convince Cassady to help them find Erek and the others. After twenty years as a newsman, Blannon considered himself a fair judge of character, but he didn't blame Gillie for harboring doubts.

Blannon knew that if he had misread Cassady's motives, he and Gillie could be in deep trouble.

They stopped at the second floor landing so Blannon could catch his breath. Blannon found himself wondering about something. "How do you know Cassady's office is in the navigation section?"

"The commset we built," Gillie answered. "We listened in on some intraship calls. One of Colonel Cassady's men mentioned the location of his office."

"And you happened to remember where it was?"

Gillie grinned and looked a little embarrassed. "Actually, we were listening for it. Joby wanted to kidnap Cassady and make him take us back home."

"Good thing for Cassady she didn't try it." Blannon grunted as he pushed himself to his feet. "Let's go."

Gillie had studied the layout of this area before. From the third-level stairway he led the way through a series of service corridors that kept them out of the main traffic areas. It took them another fifteen minutes to reach the navigation section. By luck, Cassady's office was located at the end of a hallway that branched off from the main corridor. Blannon and Gillie stopped when they were still a few meters from the intersecting hallway that led down to the office.

"I'll scout ahead and make sure there's nobody around," Gillie whispered.

While Gillie crept forward, Blannon waited against the wall and considered how he should approach Cassady. He had watched enough tough-guy shows on the holovid to know that routine, but he wasn't sure if it would work with a man like Cassady. An appeal to reason was worth a try, but considering the mental state Cassady must be in by now, trying to be reasonable could be a long shot. If nothing else worked, he could use the information he'd gotten out of his notepad. Hard to say what reaction that would provoke.

He was still thinking about it when Gillie waved him forward. He started toward the door, then stopped when Gillie frantically shook his head and pointed. It took Blannon a moment to realize Gillie was gesturing toward the sizzler tucked in Blannon's belt—the gun Joby had taken from the young sergeant on the tenth level. Blannon pulled it out and held it awkwardly as he approached the closed door. The hallway was empty, but he could hear voices from open doors only a few meters away.

Gillie glanced up at him, then turned back to press the wall plate. The door slid open and Blannon found himself staring into a small, neat office. Xavier Cassady sat behind a desk, viewing a readout screen. Blannon recognized him immediately from the holoprints he'd seen—close-cropped dark hair, gray eyes, square jaw. A young Guard lieutenant sat across from him.

The scene registered in a frozen instant of time. Then Cassady looked up in surprise and the young lieutenant came up halfway out of his chair, already twisting around and reaching for his sidearm.

"Don't!" Blannon snapped, jerking the sizzler around. A rush of adrenaline coursed through him like ice water.

The lieutenant's hand stopped on the butt of his gun. Blannon tried to keep his own weapon steady against the tremor that had started in his arm. Sweat ran down under the collar of his shirt. Had he remembered to release the gun's safety?

Cassady's quiet voice sliced through the growing tension: "Sit down, Kurt."

The lieutenant hesitated, then returned stiffly to his chair. Cassady's gray eyes moved past Blannon to fix on Gillie, then returned. His hands were on the desk, palms flat against the polished surface.

Blannon realized that he and Gillie were exposed to anyone who happened to look down the hallway. He stepped into the room and Gillie followed, locking the door behind him. Blannon finally remembered how to release the safety on the gun. He moved his thumb slowly to press the stud. The loud snap startled him.

He grinned crookedly at Cassady. Cassady did not smile back. Blannon decided it was too late for the tough-guy routine. He used his toe to snag the empty armchair and nudged it around.

"Come over here and sit down, Colonel." Blannon didn't know if panic buttons existed in real life, but he decided he'd feel better if Cassady were farther from his desk.

Cassady silently rose and stepped around the desk to sit stiffly in the armchair. Blannon noticed Cassady's holstered handgun and asked both men for their weapons. Gillie collected them and returned to stand in front of the door.

Blannon said: "My name is—"

"I know who you are," Cassady interrupted in a flat, dry voice. "Victor told me about you. I assume you're responsible for the damaged solar panel?"

Blannon nodded toward Gillie. "The boy did it. Pretty impressive, eh?"

"It doesn't matter. A crew of stasis techs are already working on the panel controls. Another window will open in less than an hour. They'll have it repaired by then." Cassady paused, studying Blannon's face. "You may think this is a game, but it isn't. Victor's men have orders to kill you on sight."

Blannon was ready with a snappy comeback, then he thought about Erek and the others and the retort faded. He moved around the desk and sat down in Cassady's swivel chair, keeping the sizzler trained at a point midway between Cassady and the lieutenant.

"Some friends of ours came across to this hub structure," he said. "A young black girl and a tall boy with blond hair. And my pilot, Erek Speros. Do you know where they are?"

"Speros was on the flight deck earlier. Victor's men took him for questioning, along with one of the stasis techs—"

"A stasis tech?" Blannon asked sharply. That wasn't part of the plan. "Troy has them?"

"Not anymore. Your two young friends rescued them. I don't know where they've gone. Troy's still looking for them." Cassady paused, watching Blannon. "The same rules apply to them. They are to be killed on sight."

"Even the kids? Would you let that happen?"

"Even if I wanted to, I couldn't stop it. Victor Troy can do pretty much as he pleases. There are thirty-five brigs aboard this ship, all armed. I have fourteen men."

"You're saying fourteen guardsmen can't beat the pants off thirty-five brigs?"

Cassady smiled thinly. "It isn't that simple."

"But . . . " Blannon stopped. Cassady sat deadly silent, his face as cold and hard as the face of an ice sculpture. If Blannon were wrong about Cassady, it meant that he and Gillie had risked their lives for nothing. Then he realized Cassady was wearing a full-dress Guard uniform, with several medals and commendation ribbons arranged neatly on the left side of his chest. The uniform fit perfectly—not only the tailoring, but also the attitude with which it was worn.

Cassady doesn't look like a man turned traitor, he thought. He decided to find out.

"A lot has been said about you in the past few weeks, Colonel. Not much of it has been complimentary—"

"I'm not here to win a popularity contest."

Blannon continued, watching Cassady carefully: "I don't think you're the kind of man who wants to be responsible for children getting killed."

"I don't need a lecture on moral obligations," Cassady snapped. "Those kids shouldn't be on this ship. That was their own doing."

"Do they deserve to die for a mistake like that?"

The muscle along Cassady's jaw stiffened, but he remained silent.

"I know you're planning to take this ship to Kisatchie." Again, Blannon watched for a reaction. There was none from Cassady; the lieutenant shifted uneasily in his chair. "I think I've figured out what kind of deal you made with Troy. Troy wants to get his brother out of Kisatchie, and the rest of his men. That's his first step in putting his brig organization back together."

No response. Blannon went on: "What I couldn't figure out was what you and your men would gain. At first I was convinced Troy had some kind of hold on you. But I couldn't find anything that made sense. The only other possibility was that you and Troy were going into business together. As theories go, that isn't so far-fetched. With the *Wasp* and those interstream missiles, you could set up the biggest brig operation in Omega."

Even that provoked no reaction. Blannon leaned back in the chair and put his feet on the desk. "But *why?* That was the question. Why would you throw away a distinguished career with the Guard to become a brig leader? You're a decent man, Colonel. And your men seem decent enough, despite what they've done." Blannon shook his head. "You wouldn't team up with a snake like Victor Troy."

Cassady's face remained devoid of expression. Blannon maintained a stolid silence, determined this time to draw Cassady out. When at last Cassady spoke, he used the same hard, flat voice as before:

"We have no intention of joining Troy's brig organization. Our effort now is aimed toward one goal. After that, Troy will go his way and we'll go ours."

"And your goal?"

"The gold reserves on Sierra."

Blannon carefully avoided showing the astonishment he felt. "You can do that with the *Wasp?*"

"With its interstream missiles, and a few connections on Sierra."

Blannon pursed his lips thoughtfully. Sierra was the seat of UNSA government—the most heavily guarded planet in the stream. The gold reserves stored in Sierra's underground vaults were the basis of UNSA script used on all developed planets.

"But that would be a big operation," he said. "You knew you would need more than fourteen men. That's why you invited Troy to join you."

Cassady nodded. "I knew he had gone to the Malachi Bloc. It wasn't too difficult to find him. I convinced him that a temporary partnership would help each of us. Unfortunately, most of his men are imprisoned on Kisatchie. We have to get them out before we can act."

A long silence followed. Cassady stared at Blannon with eyes the color of graymetal.

"The Sierra gold," Blannon said slowly. "An ambitious project to say the least. And after the heist is over, you and Troy will shake hands, split the booty, and go on your merry ways?"

Cassady must have detected the skepticism in Blannon's voice. "Did you ever serve in the Guard, Mr. Blannon?"

Blannon shook his head.

"It's been twenty years for me," Cassady went on. He inclined his head toward the lieutenant. "Kurt has six years' service. Most of that time we've spent chasing brigs. As you can probably imagine, it isn't easy to track unregistered streamers through the Fringe, so the brigs usually get away. If we're lucky enough to grab a brig leader, chances are he'll get off on a legal technicality —a minor slip by the Guard when they ran him down and arrested him. There are so many complicated rules it's almost impossible to arrest a brig leader and bring him to court. If he's put away, it's for maybe five years or so, then he's free to continue where he left off." He shrugged. "When you've seen that scenario played over as many times as we have, you begin to wonder if a guardsman's salary is enough to make it worth going through again."

"So you decided to give yourself a bonus."

Cassady stared at Blannon, then offered a wry smile.

"You newsmen are all alike. You insist on cutting through the rhetoric right to the bone." He waved a hand. "Maybe we're doing this out of pure and simple greed. That's the ultimate motivator, I suppose."

"That *isn't* why we're doing it!"

Blannon's eyes jerked to the young lieutenant. The words had burst out of his mouth as if under pressure.

"What is it, then?" he asked.

Hollins glanced at Cassady. When Cassady gave a slight shrug of his shoulders, he turned back to Blannon. "We want to establish our own Guard unit on the Fringe."

With a jolt, Blannon realized what the lieutenant was getting at. "That's your plan, to set yourself up as Fringe vigilantes?"

The lieutenant colored slightly. "Call it what you want. The Guard is spread too thin out there. The Fringe has turned into a shooting range. Thousands of people—women and children, too—have been massacred." He waved his hands. "Most of them are dirt poor, but the brigs don't care. They'll murder an entire family without blinking an eye if it'll get them a few credits' worth of merchandise." He paused long enough to take a breath. "We have to give the Fringe some protection and we have to let the brigs know they can't attack Fringe settlements with impunity."

"You think one small group of ex-guardsmen can do that?"

"Yes! We won't be shackled by rules and regulations that give all the advantage to the brigs. When we get a call for help, we'll be ready and we'll hit the brigs before they can get their ships into the stream. That's the only way to run them down, but we can't do it if we have to follow every rule to the letter."

Blannon's eyes moved back to Cassady. "Quite a partnership. Troy contributes the men and you contribute the hardware. You raid Sierra and split the loot. Troy uses his share to rebuild his brig operation, and you use yours to set up a vigilante group to chase brigs." He paused. "You have to admit there's a touch of irony there."

"Troy doesn't know about our plans," Cassady said evenly. "But what we're doing here doesn't alter the basic facts: If Troy begins raiding Fringe planets again, we'll be after him."

Another long silence fell over them. Blannon studied Cassady's face, his mind going back to the information he'd gotten from his notepad. He saw the dark smudges under Cassady's eyes and felt a sudden surge of understanding for what the man was going through.

He decided the cat-and-mouse game had gone far enough.

"You lay out a good line, Colonel. Especially the part about Sierra. I'm sure Troy's mouth waters when he thinks about all that gold. Maybe his greed has blinded him to the absurdity of the notion that you would really try to steal it."

Cassady opened his mouth to say something, but Blannon cut him off.

"You would never give a man like Victor Troy a chance to get a new operation going. Never. The idea goes against everything you've stood for. And besides, I don't believe greed is the ultimate motivator. As a newsman, I've had firsthand experience with human actions ranging from selfless heroics to the most despicable back-stabbing acts of malice you can imagine. I've seen what a man can do to another man if he has the right monkey on his back, and I know of something that can push a man a lot farther than greed. A monkey with claws and sharp teeth."

Cassady waited, tight-lipped.

"Revenge," Blannon said. "It can eat at a man, make him half crazy." He paused, watching Cassady closely. "I know about Mlissa and James Robert."

Cassady's face went stark white. He jumped out of his chair and leaned over the desk to glare at Blannon, ignoring the weapon in Blannon's hand. "You have no right to—"

"Killed on Giant Forest by Troy's brother," Blannon plunged ahead, trying to ignore the murderous look in Cassady's eyes. The young lieutenant sat ramrod straight in his chair, his eyes fixed on Blannon. "I also know that Mlissa wasn't your sister. I checked the travel records. Over the past five years you made sixty-two trips to see Mlissa and James Robert on Giant Forest, but only four to your parents' homeworld of Cambridge. Clearly, you considered Giant Forest your home more than Cambridge—"

"That's enough," Cassady said, the words forced through clenched teeth. "I'll—"

"Mlissa was your wife," Blannon went on. "And James Robert was your son. You kept the marriage a secret out of concern for their safety. I'm sure you blame yourself for what happened." He stared evenly at Cassady. "You don't have any intention of breaking Emil Troy and the rest of the brigs out of the penal colony. You want to kill them."

Chapter 17

DIANA switched off the commset and swiveled around to Erek. "They're coming. In force."

"How soon?"

"The next skip window from Semegen IV will open in"—she turned to consult the information still glowing on the readout screen—"two hours and seventeen minutes. The unit commander said they'd come through that window."

Erek released a long breath. The window to Kisatchie would open in barely half an hour—long before the Guard unit could get here. If Cassady's men were still monitoring interstream messages from the seventh-level CommSec office, they would know about Diana's call to Semegen IV. Cassady would also realize that his only hope of getting out of here before the Guard arrived would be to get into the emergency command center and set up the skip for that next window.

Somehow Erek and Diana would have to keep him out until that window passed.

"We'd better get ready," he said.

The best cover in the ECC was offered by the low wall that surrounded the command module. The wall was heavy graymetal: It would deflect pellets and sizzler beams and maybe even carbine blasts.

Still, Erek hesitated. If he and Diana took cover behind the wall, the command module would be directly behind them. Any fire coming at them from the perimeter of the room could be potentially lethal to the command module. If it were disabled—

Something crashed against the outer sealing door and their options suddenly ran out. He closed the security door and he and Diana crouched behind the waist-high wall. Another thud jarred the sealing door.

Xavier Cassady returned slowly to the chair. His eyes went to the young lieutenant and during a long moment of silence Blannon was aware that something passed between the two men. When Cassady turned back to Blannon, his face had undergone a transformation that replaced the blue ice in his eyes with a deep weariness. His voice was calm.

"Giant Forest is at the far edge of the Fringe. I told Mlissa it wasn't safe there for her and James Robert. But Giant Forest was her home, and her parents' home." A shadow of pain crossed his face. "I didn't insist. After all, she shouldn't have to leave her home-world because of our marriage."

"The only alternative was to make sure nobody knew they were there," Blannon said.

"Kurt knew." Cassady nodded toward the lieutenant. "And a few of my men. But there was no official record, not even with the Guard. I was captain of a Fringe patrol ship. As you pointed out, it would have been too easy to get to me through Mlissa and James Robert." His voice changed there at the end; he had to clear his throat before he went on. "Jock Clyatt and Emil Troy were after kicks and booty when they raided

Giant Forest. That was their style. It was a fluke that they hit the town where Mlissa and James Robert lived." Again he paused. "They got what they wanted, then razed the town. No reason. Just to have a good time. To this day, they don't realize they killed my wife and son."

Blannon nodded thoughtfully. "Of course, Victor Troy would have no way of knowing."

Cassady offered a wry smile. "A few months later, Troy's brother and some of his men were caught in a Guard net. We got lucky that time—they were found guilty and sentenced to Kisatchie. But not for the raid on Giant Forest. They were convicted for transporting stolen merchandise. Nobody could pin the raid on them. Five years, maximum. Then they'll be out."

"How do you know they're the ones who hit Giant Forest? There was speculation, but—"

"I have my sources. Nothing that could be admitted as evidence in a court." Again came the wry smile. "Legal technicalities." The smile vanished. "But there is no doubt that Emil Troy and Jock Clyatt murdered my family."

"And you don't want to wait five years to get at them. You want them now."

"Wouldn't you?"

Blannon didn't want to think about a question like that. "Why did you need Victor Troy? If you wanted to get back at his brother and this man Clyatt, why not go to the penal colony and do it yourself?"

"There are a thousand Guard personnel on Kisatchie, and ten thousand prisoners. My quarrel is with Emil Troy and Jock Clyatt and forty-three others. I can't simply land on Kisatchie and start blazing away. And interstream missiles are not selective weapons."

Blannon understood. "You've figured out a way to break them out without launching a full-scale attack on the planet."

"Troy has a communication link with his men on

Kisatchie. He contacted them and had them set it up from there so he can land and pick them up all as a group. I told him I wouldn't go along with wholesale slaughter. He wants his people back, so he agreed."

"Kisatchie security will let you through?"

"Hardly. We'll use the *Wasp* to knock out the perimeter defenses. They're remote, so we can do that without endangering security personnel. Then Troy will land on the planet with his own ship and pick up his people."

"His ship is docked here?"

Cassady nodded. "In a hangar in the portside cylinder."

That was the part Blannon hadn't figured out. Now he was sure he knew the rest of it. "When Troy's men are all on his ship, you'll use the *Wasp* to blast it out of existence."

"That's what they deserve," Cassady said tersely. "But it isn't my style. I'll give them a fair fight. The *Wasp* against Troy's ship. Conventional weapons, not the interstream missiles."

"Very noble," Blannon said dryly. "But you're forgetting something. The penal authorities on Kisatchie will call for help the instant you attack their perimeter defense. Do you think the Guard will stand by and let you and Troy duel it out?"

"The Guard won't be able to reach Kisatchie."

Blannon frowned. "Why not?"

"*Copernicus* will be blocking the Kisatchie focal point."

Then Blannon remembered what Erek had said about the focal point with the double set of coordinates. *Two ships can't go through it at the same time.*

"What will stop the Guard from blowing *Copernicus* out of the way?" Then Blannon saw the answer. "They know the stasis techs are aboard. They're your insurance."

Cassady nodded. "I know the Guard commander at

Semegen IV. He won't attack *Copernicus* as long as the technicians are aboard. After we've dealt with Troy, we'll skip directly through the stream from the focal point. The Guard won't be able to track us."

"Assuming you win the battle."

Cassady accepted the point with a shrug.

Blannon leaned back in his chair. "You never intended to go after the gold reserves on Sierra."

Cassady glanced at the lieutenant beside him, brought his eyes back to Blannon. "Even a ship like the *Wasp* couldn't break through the Sierra defenses. That part was for Troy. We had to give him something his greedy little heart could believe."

"Your men know that?"

Cassady nodded.

"And they still went along with this? They know they'll never be able to go back to the Guard."

"They're all good men." Cassady's voice deepened. He cleared his throat. "Avery, McLaughlin, Asusa, Dorland, Williams—all of them are the finest men an officer could hope to command. They know what happened to Mlissa and James Robert, and they know that the Fringe will become a wasteland unless somebody steps in to stop what's happening."

"So you really intend to become vigilantes?"

Cassady frowned. "I don't like the term, Mr. Blannon. But we intend to set up our own independent Guard unit. We don't need the Sierra gold to do it. We'll have the *Wasp* and the Fringe worlds will be grateful for our help. They'll fund us—"

The buzzing of the console interrupted him. He turned in surprise to look at the readout screen. Beside him, Lieutenant Hollins stiffened perceptibly. The screen lighted with a line of gibberish.

"What's that mean?" Blannon asked.

"Coded message." Cassady reached across the desk, swung the keyboard around to his side, and punched in several quick commands. The look on his face changed from surprise to disbelief as new information flowed across the screen. "Something's happened on the flight deck. The command module . . . " He frowned and studied the information again as if he doubted the words he'd almost spoken. He looked up at Blannon. "It's been deactivated." Then, more sharply: "Is Speros responsible for that?"

"That wasn't in the plan," Blannon said. "Anyway, you said he left the flight deck hours ago."

Cassady's eyes returned to the screen. "Operating control of the ship has switched to the emergency command center on the twentieth level. Somebody's up there."

Blannon's brow pulled down. Things were happening too fast. "Troy?"

Cassady shook his head. "He's got control of the flight deck. I haven't challenged him on that. He wouldn't have any reason to shift control to the ECC."

"Must be Erek, then. Can we get in touch with him?"

Cassady was already pulling the deskset around. He keyed a quick series of numbers into the keypad, then punched the speaker bar for audio. A moment later, the deskset beeped.

"This is Xavier Cassady. Who is this?"

No answer. Cassady repeated the question. Still nothing.

"Let me try," Blannon suggested. He called out to the commset: "Erek, is that you? This is Leo."

After a moment a voice answered: "Leo? Where are you?"

"Colonel Cassady's office."

"Cassady's office! How—"

"It's a long story. What are you doing up there?"

It took a few minutes to get the explanations made. Then Blannon heard a loud *crack!* in the background and a woman's voice close to the commset.

"Who's in there with you?" he asked.

"Her name's Diana Wells. She's—" Erek paused.

Blannon heard more sounds that he couldn't identify. "The brigs are breaking through the door. I have to get behind cover." The speaker clicked and went dead.

"We'd better get up there," Blannon said. "Sounds like they're in trouble."

"We're all in trouble," Cassady said grimly. "With the flight deck disabled, the ECC is the ship's operations coordinator. If the command module in there is damaged, this ship will be totally out of control. That includes the environmental control system. What in God's name is Speros doing up there?"

"If there's an interstream commset, he probably used it to call for help."

Cassady's eyes widened. He turned back to the terminal and keyed in a quick series of commands. The readout screen blinked through several frames before it reached the information he wanted. After he'd read it, he leaned back in the chair with a heavy sigh.

"A message was punched through to Semegen IV ten minutes ago." He glanced at the chronometer that was inset in the lower left corner of the screen, then turned to the lieutenant. "Get some men up to the twentieth level as fast as you can."

Hollins nodded and rose from his chair.

"Wait," Blannon ordered. He turned the sizzler on the lieutenant, but his eyes remained on Cassady. "Are you still going to try to take the ship through that window?"

"If I can," Cassady answered bluntly. "I can still make it before the Guard gets here. But first we have to get into the ECC and give the order to the drive system." He looked past Blannon at the wall chronometer. "The window will open in twenty minutes."

"I can't let you go, then," Blannon said to the lieutenant. He held the gun steady. "Erek's up there, and—"

"You fool," Cassady said harshly. "Don't you think Troy knows that call went out to Semegen IV?"

Blannon shook his head in confusion. "I don't see how—"

"Troy knows he has to get the ship through that next window. That's his only chance to reach Kisatchie. He won't let anything stop him from getting into the ECC." Cassady's lips thinned. "At least my men don't kill children. But I can guarantee that Troy will kill anyone who tries to stop him."

Blannon stared at him. Then he let the gun drop to his side. The lieutenant turned quickly and left the room.

Victor Troy rushed down the corridor toward the ECC with Klaus Burdick trailing in his wake. Several of his men had gathered in a knot outside the sealing door.

"What is going on here?" he demanded.

The knot unraveled and the men cast shifty-eyed looks at one another. Nobody wanted to be the one to tell him the bad news.

"*I want answers!*" Troy screamed shrilly.

The men fell back, staring at him. Troy clenched his teeth, breathing hard. He had to keep himself under control or this entire operation could fall apart. He glanced down at his wristwatch. Burdick had assured him that the drive system was still intact and functioning. All they had to do was get to the command module and order it to take the ship through that window. But they would have to do it within the next fifteen minutes if they hoped to get through before the Guard arrived.

"It's locked from the inside," one of the men ventured. He held a huge prybar. Troy could see the marks on the door where they had been trying to force it open. He felt his pulse pounding in his ears and had to take a few deep breaths to keep his rage from boiling over. Did they really think they could force open a sealing door with a prybar?

Troy snatched a long-barreled carbine from one of the men and set it for a tight focus. Used right, a weapon like that would produce nearly as much power as a laser torch. He shouldered his way through to the sealing door and looked it over, then stepped back two meters and trained the carbine directly on one of the big hinges.

Something inside the door snapped and it sagged outward. The edge glowed white, quickly cooling to red. Erek released a short burst of pellets that rattled against the graymetal. Somebody behind the door cursed and ducked back. A moment later he saw the end of a prybar working on the door and the gap widened. This time a sizzler beam slanted through the opening and passed a meter over Erek's head. As he ducked, he saw a man in brown fatigues slip through the door in a crouching run and take cover behind a work-station unit near the outer wall. A moment later, more sizzler fire snapped against the wall beside Erek and another man slipped through the door.

"They'll surround us," Diana, behind him, said quietly. She sounded remarkably calm. Erek knew she was right; the work-station units would give good cover to the brigs as they moved around the room.

He used his pellet gun to fire short bursts, hoping to keep more men from coming through the door. But when the sizzler fire homed in on him and crackled along the top of the wall, he had to duck.

Despite his efforts to stop them, Erek knew after several minutes that at least a dozen brigs had slipped through the door and moved around to both sides of the room. Then he heard a shout and the sizzler fire stopped.

"There's no need for anyone to get hurt." Erek recognized Victor Troy's voice from someplace near the back wall. "All you have to do is throw down your weapons and come out. You have my word."

Erek glanced over his shoulder. Diana had moved back to the opposite side of the security wall to watch that side of the room. He turned back and waited, watching the door. A moment later, another order was given from far back against the outer wall and the overhead lights went out. Erek hunched down as the brigs at the far perimeter began firing. The darkness gave way to a dazzling blue light show.

Chapter 18

JOBY didn't know what an emergency command center looked like, but she was confident she could find it. According to Diana, the ECC was on the twentieth level out near the hub. It took Joby and Richard only a few minutes to climb to the twentieth level and find the main corridor that curved around the cylinder. This part of the ship was quiet—looked deserted, in fact—and when Joby heard raised voices and other commotion down a branching passage, she knew she was close to the action.

She tapped Richard's shoulder and held a finger to her lips, then led the way down the passage.

Erek had told her and Richard to go back to the basement after they junked the command processor on the flight deck. Joby hadn't argued with him, but neither did she intend to follow his instructions. She had already learned that Erek was far from experienced at fighting brigs. He and Diana would need help up here.

Down the corridor, Joby saw a few brigs huddled outside a partly open door. She and Richard moved over

close to the wall and stopped. As she watched, two of
the brigs slipped through the door. Joby could hear the
faint crackle of sizzler fire coming from inside the
darkened room. That meant Erek and Diana were still
alive. It also meant they were in trouble.

Another few minutes passed before Joby decided the
four brigs still in the passageway were going to stay
there. Maybe they had been left to guard the entrance.
If so, they were doing a poor job, crouched there peering through the door with their rear ends hanging out.
More likely they had decided to stay out here where it
was safe.

She could guess from the sounds of the carbine and
sizzler fire that there were at least ten or twelve brigs
already inside the ECC. Somehow, she and Richard
would have to sneak inside without drawing their attention. Maybe they could get in position to catch the brigs
in a crossfire and keep them busy long enough for Erek
and Diana to escape.

Her eyes went back to the four men at the door. First
things first . . .

With rapid movement of her fingers, she told Richard
what she wanted to do. Then she put a supply of steel
balls in her mouth, edged around the corner, and crept
as close as she dared to the four brigs in the corridor.

She drew back and let the first ball fly, reloading
before the man fell. She got the next one when he turned
with a look of surprise and the third as he brought his
gun up. The fourth man was able to snap off a shot with
his sidearm before Joby's steel ball punched him between the eyes, but the beam missed her by at least six
inches.

They were out cold when she checked them. Richard
dragged them a few meters down the corridor as Joby
crept closer to the doorway and peered through. As her
eyes adjusted to the darkness, she began to get an idea
of what was happening. Erek and Diana were pinned
down in the middle of the room. That was where the

whir and chatter of the pellet gun was coming from. She couldn't see what they were using for cover, but she was pretty sure the main control unit was in there somewhere. The brigs had split up to attack them from both sides. Most of them had taken cover behind the work stations that formed a long curve along the left side. Joby could hear Troy shouting orders over there.

Joby knew she had been wrong in her first guess: There were a lot more than ten or twelve brigs in here. The idea of a simple crossfire was out. But the layout of the room suggested another possibility: If she and Richard could sneak in on the right side and keep from getting shot long enough to take out the brigs over there, maybe they could clear a way out for Erek and Diana. From there they should be able to use the workstation units for cover and get back to the door without exposing themselves to the larger group on the other side.

Joby used her hands to explain the idea to Richard. Then, keeping close to the floor, they slipped silently through the door. Two men had taken cover behind a work station just to the right of the door. They were on their knees, peering over the desk unit with their guns resting on the flat surface of the console shelf. Their attention was centered on the green glow that came from the command module, and Joby was able to get within three meters of them before she released her sling. One of the men grunted and went down; the second barely had time to turn toward her with a surprised look on his face before the steel ball knocked him senseless.

Didn't expect anyone from this side, did you? She grinned with satisfaction. Both men were out cold; at this range that didn't surprise her. Only one man crouched behind the next work station. With all the crackling sizzler fire and the chatter of the pellet gun, he hadn't heard his friends go down only a few meters away. He was lining the sights of his gun up on the command module when Joby let the steel ball fly. He slumped down without a sound. Joby got the two men at the next work station so easily she almost felt disappointed. This was nothing more than target practice.

She and Richard crawled forward on their bellies toward the last work station on this side of the room. Beyond it Joby could see an open area filled with dark shapes that she thought were chairs and tables. Lined up against the back wall were several of those machines that dropped packaged food into a tray when you pushed the right buttons.

She paused to rethink her plan. This side of the room would be clear after she got the three men who were huddled behind the last work station. With Richard covering her, she could sneak up to that wall and help Erek and Diana slip out. The command module and the wall would hide her from the brigs on the other side of the room. With luck, she could get Erek and Diana completely out of the room before Troy and the others even knew what was happening.

But luck turned against her. As she positioned herself for a shot, one of the brigs happened to turn his head slightly and spotted her. She got off a shot that put him down, but not before he shouted a warning. The other two spun around, bringing their guns up. Joby knew she would be cut in half before she could get both of them. She scrambled for cover behind a work station as Richard's gun exploded twice. Then he rolled in beside her.

Kurt Hollins and his men had nearly reached the corridor leading to the ECC when he heard the two explosions. He sprinted toward the corridor with his men close behind, sure that when he reached the ECC he would find a smoking ruin.

He rounded the corner and almost stumbled over four brigs that were laid out neatly against the wall. Dead or unconscious—he didn't take the time to find out which. The ECC was dark, punctuated by bright blue sizzler

flashes. Through the door he could make out the hulk-
ing shapes of work stations and a green glow near the
center that must have come from the command module's readout screen. Crackling sizzler fire was punctuated with the chatter of a pellet gun. Another sharp
explosion was followed by a shouted order from the opposite side of the room. Troy, he thought.

Kurt eased himself through the door, conscious of the
bright light behind him. It took only a moment for the
rest of his men to slip inside and spread themselves out
along the wall. Kurt had never before found himself in a
situation exactly like this, but he had fought brigs long
enough to know their tactics. By the time his eyes had
fully adjusted to the darkness, he had sorted out the
chaos in the ECC and formed a plan. The brigs were
fighting in two separate areas. At least twenty of them
had taken cover on the left side of the room and were
concentrating their fire on the command module.
Speros and the stasis tech must have gotten pinned
behind the security wall. A smaller battle was taking
place farther back along the wall on the right side, near
the lounge. Kurt was relieved to see that the lingering
blue smoke was heaviest there and hadn't come from
the command area.

Kurt's first priority was clear: He had to stop the
brigs from firing those sizzler beams toward the command module. One stray shot could turn the control
processor into scrap metal.

Using hand signals, he ordered Captain Asusa and
three of his men to begin working their way around the
perimeter to the right side of the door, then he and the
rest of his men crept to the left, toward two shadowy
forms that were huddled behind the nearest work
station. With all the noise and confusion, the brigs were
unaware that he and his men had even entered the ECC.

Kurt hesitated, then thumbed the control on his
sizzler to low power. The first man went down, but the
reduced charge didn't take quickly enough on the other

one, and he let out a yell before he crumpled to the deck. The two brigs at the next work station scrambled around behind the unit with their sizzlers winking bright blue. Kurt hit one of them, then dropped and rolled across the floor to the next station with sizzler beams popping all around him. Not low power, that.

At Kurt's signal, one of his men farther back darted to a work station in the inner row. From there he got the two brigs easily. Kurt edged forward to the next work station and they repeated the procedure with the same effect. The air heated with the crackling of sizzler fire. Behind Kurt, one of his men grunted and fell; he didn't turn to see who had gotten hit. A beam grazed his arm, burning away a strip of cloth and searing his skin.

Kurt knew that eventually he and his men would rout the brigs, but he also knew it was taking too long. He began to push harder, driving the brigs back toward the lounge. One went down, then another. Several made a break for the inner circle of work stations. Kurt's men had been waiting for that and picked them off easily.

From the other side of the room came the steady snap of sizzler fire and an occasional shattering explosion. Kurt knew what was causing the explosions—he had heard about the boy in the basement with the big pistol. Not a pellet gun, but an old-style projectile weapon that used explosive powder. Kurt wasn't sure which side the boy was fighting for, but the gun added to the general confusion and worked to Kurt's advantage.

A sizzler beam raked across the work-station shelf in front of him. He lifted his head to fire back and ducked again under a new barrage. He saw several brigs duck across the open space to the inner ring of work stations. During a flash of blue fire, he caught a glimpse of Victor Troy's scarred face and realized that Troy was making a break for the door. He twisted around and signaled two of his men to intercept, but they were pinned by the heavy fire. Kurt saw one of them take a sizzler beam in the chest and go down—Avery, he thought—and the brigs pushed through to the outer perimeter of work stations. Kurt got two of them before they passed out of his sight. Then he was forced to turn his attention back to the brigs who were still holding ground near the lounge.

The battle lasted a few more minutes, but the remaining brigs were outclassed and knew it. After Kurt and his men had stunned half a dozen, the others began throwing out their guns.

With one of his men herding prisoners back toward the door, Kurt and the others doubled back and netted three more brigs hiding inside a small office along the outer wall. By the time they returned to the entrance, the ECC was quiet except for sporadic shooting from the far side of the room. Kurt sent one of his men back to check on Avery and the others who were wounded, then began making his way toward the sounds of gunfire.

He had nearly reached the lounge before he found Captain Asusa and his two men crouched down behind a work station. One of them nursed an ugly bruise on his forearm, cursing steadily in a low voice.

"We got the brigs," Asusa said. He hooked a thumb toward the lounge and said with a disgusted tone, "As far as I can tell, it's the two kids from the basement. They won't let us get any closer."

Kurt craned his neck to call out and ducked as a steel ball sliced through the air an inch above his head.

"Wait," he shouted. "We're guardsmen—"

He jerked back as another steel ball whistled past his right ear and shattered something behind him.

"You'll be dead guardsmen if you come any closer!" the girl yelled back in a shrill voice.

"Colonel Cassady sent us to help—" he began, then ducked again. He turned wearily to put his back against the work station. Two dozen brigs hadn't been able to stop them as effectively as a young girl with a sling.

Then a man's voice came from the command module

in the middle of the room: "Let them through, Joby."

Silence. Then: "You sure?"

"Yeah."

After another brief pause, the girl spoke grudgingly. "All right, come ahead."

Kurt ordered his men to holster their weapons, then he rose up from behind the work station and made his way cautiously toward the lounge. In the glow of the command module, he could see the girl's black eyes watching him steadily as he approached. She did not put down her sling. The boy stood beside her, blue smoke curling from the big gun in his hand.

Kurt turned toward the command module as a man of about his own age stepped through the opening, followed by a young woman. Kurt was relieved to see that she wore the uniform of a stasis technician.

"Is the command system intact?" he asked.

She nodded. "You'd better get some technicians up here from the flight deck."

Kurt nodded and opened his communicator to make the call. Then he glanced down at his wristwatch and saw that they had missed the stream window by six minutes. He felt something close to relief, and at the same time a deep weariness settled over him. He had visited Giant Forest many times with Colonel Cassady, and Mlissa and James Robert had made him feel a part of their family. Destruction and death on the Fringe worlds—that was what Colonel Cassady wanted to stop.

He thought about Avery and Williams and the others who had already died.

Then he shook away the sense of loss with a slight shrug of his shoulders. Colonel Cassady still needed him.

He opened the communicator to make his call.

Chapter 19

VICTOR Troy ran down the narrow hallway with his heart pounding and his breath coming in short gasps. Klaus Burdick was close behind him, with Jimmy Mosby and Raj Alton trailing by a few meters. Only the four of them had managed to slip past the guardsmen and get out of the ECC. When Troy used his communicator to call for his men on the flight deck, he found them engaged in a fight with guardsmen who had somehow boxed them in. No help would be coming from them.

He reached the stairway he'd been looking for, slammed through the door, and started up with Burdick and the others close on his heels.

The fury that had nearly consumed him at the ECC had been replaced now by a cold determination. He had accepted the fact that his plans to break Emil and the rest of his men out of Kisatchie were ruined. For the time being, at least. But the grand prize was still within reach. He'd had his eye on it from the moment Xavier

Cassady approached him with his scheme. He would not let it slip away.

The stairway opened onto another corridor that would take them directly to the hangar. Troy had covered half its length when the door at the far end slid open and three men in black and gray stepped through. The guardsmen looked as surprised as Troy. They obviously hadn't expected to find him this close to the hangar.

Before they had time to react, Troy's sizzler spurted blue fire. One of the men buckled and went down, clutching his midsection. Another jerked back against the wall and fell as Burdick's carbine cut him nearly in half. The third reached cover behind the partly open door and began returning fire.

Troy stood his ground in the middle of the corridor with his feet apart and his thumb jammed on the firing stud, paying no attention to the fire that snapped in the air all around him. He felt a savage heat rush out of him to merge with the energy beam from his weapon.

Then the guardsman was down.

"Come on!" Troy ran past the slumped body into the graymetal cavern of the starboard hangar.

"There she is," Burdick gasped from behind him.

"*Quiet!*" Troy stood still for a moment, listening. The hangar was silent. Twelve meters away, the *Wasp* waited on its landing strip—sleek, deadly. With a ship like that under his command, the Guard would never run him down. His eyes went to the missile ports just in front of the swept-back portside wing. His heart pounded, but this time from anticipation rather than exertion. The *Wasp*'s armory held thirty interstream missiles—thirty of the deadliest weapons known to man. With them, Troy could strike a target from the safety of an adjoining stream sector and escape with no danger of being tracked.

He had already decided how he would use several of those missiles—

A door slid open. Troy spun around in time to see Xavier Cassady and three uniformed men step into the hangar from an elevator ten meters away. Troy fired instantly, slicing one of the guardsmen across the chest. Cassady and the others ducked back into the elevator.

Troy made a dash for the cover of the *Wasp*'s landing struts. Boots pounded behind him as Burdick and the others followed. He threw himself behind the starboard strut and Burdick crowded in behind him. Raj Alton turned to fire at the elevator, then twisted and fell with a sizzler burn in his throat. Jimmy Mosby dived behind the nearby flange of the landing strip.

"We can't stay here," Burdick said.

Troy knew he was right. The *Wasp*'s boarding ladder was on the port side. Cassady had probably already called for help, and if reinforcements entered the hangar from the other side, they would catch Troy and the others in a lethal crossfire. Then he would never reach that ladder.

He motioned to Mosby.

"We have to get over to the other side," he said in a low voice. He nodded toward the guardsmen inside the elevator. "Keep them busy until Burdick and I get up that ladder."

Mosby brandished his carbine. "Sure." Then he frowned. "How will I get up?"

"When we get inside the ship we'll turn the tribarrel on them," Troy said. "That'll take care of them."

Mosby grinned and made a circle with his thumb and forefinger and positioned himself behind the flange. Mosby wasn't bright, but he was an excellent marksman, and the short-barreled carbine made an effective weapon at this range. He was also expendable, a characteristic which did not describe Klaus Burdick. Burdick had been a pilot in the Guard before he joined Troy five years ago. He was the only one who could fly the *Wasp*.

Troy waited for Mosby's carbine to open up, then he and Burdick broke from cover at the same time and ducked under the ship's belly. From behind them came the steady thunderclap of Mosby's gun. Then they had reached the shelter of the port side.

Troy looked up along the boarding ladder mounted flush against the gleaming black hull. High above him, the hatch cover stood open. The ship's fuselage blocked it from the view of the men in the elevator. If Mosby could keep them pinned there a few more minutes . . .

Troy holstered his sizzler, grasped the ladder rails, and started up. He had barely reached the halfway point when he heard a shout. He turned his head to look out past the wing. Four guardsmen had spilled out of a service stairway at the far wall. Jimmy Mosby was frantically backing toward the corridor behind him, alternating his carbine blasts between the two groups of guardsmen. He cast a single plaintive look up at Troy, then tumbled backward, flung his arms, and lay still.

Troy swore and grasped the handrails, pulling himself up the ladder as fast as he could. Burdick's pellet gun chattered briefly below him. Sizzler fire crackled against the hull all around him, but he dared not take the time to shoot back. The hatchway was just above him, almost within reach.

Burdick's pellet gun stopped abruptly and Troy heard a strangled sob, followed by the sound of a body smashing into the deck far below.

He didn't have to look back to know what had happened. Pulling himself through the hatchway, he hit the control to close the cover and scrambled to the weapons board. The burning fury had returned, but he kept it deep inside. He grasped the controls of the nose-mounted tribarrel and began to swing it toward the running guardsmen.

Erek crouched behind a supporting pylon high up on the curve from the *Wasp*. He had come out of an elevator with Lieutenant Hollins and joined Gillie and Leo Blannon where they had taken cover behind the pylon with a man he recognized as Colonel Xavier Cassady. Cassady had sent Hollins and the rest of his men back to clean out the brigs that had taken refuge in the flight deck. Erek was glad that Diana Wells had remained in the ECC to help the stasis techs get the ship's operating system back in order. Joby and Richard stayed there with them in case any stray brigs came back to the ECC.

The number of bodies that lay scattered around the hangar gave ample evidence of the degree of violence that had been dealt out in the past few minutes. Three guardsmen lay in pools of blood against the far wall. A body in brown fatigues was sprawled under the starboard wing and another brig lay dead just outside a stairwell door.

But the battle was far from over. Three guardsmen were pinned inside an elevator on the opposite side of the hangar. They had moved back into better cover—there was nothing to shoot at with Troy inside the armored cockpit of the *Wasp*—but that didn't stop Troy from raking the deck and wall around the elevator with the tribarrel from time to time. The ratcheting sound mingled with the rapid *ping-ping-ping* of ricocheting pellets.

Erek moved up closer to Xavier Cassady. "Can't you do something about that?"

Cassady shook his head grimly. "We don't have anything that will punch through the armor of that ship. Our only chance is to get inside . . . " The rest of his words were lost to another burst from the tribarrel. Then Cassady's communicator buzzed. He unclipped it from his belt and flipped it open. "Cassady."

"We've reached a standoff, Colonel." Erek recognized the clipped voice that came from the tiny speaker grille. "I don't think I have to tell you what I can do with this ship."

"I doubt you can do much," Cassady responded tersely. "Your pilot is dead. I can see him from here."

Erek realized he meant Klaus Burdick, lying at the base of the boarding ladder.

"You're wrong, Colonel. I still have an experienced pilot. Can you guess who?"

Cassady issued a harsh bark of laughter. "You expect me to fly that ship for you?"

"If you don't, I'll use the powergun to blast my way out of here. You can guess what I'll do to *Copernicus* once I'm outside."

"Assuming you can get the ship outside—"

"I've operated streamers all my life, Colonel. Believe me when I say I can operate this one well enough to break out of this hangar if you don't open the doors within five minutes."

Cassady pursed his lips, thinking. Then: "We can't do it that fast. We'll have to give the order through the ECC—"

"I want *action*," Troy rasped. "You have exactly five minutes to get in here and open that hangar door. Then I'll use the powergun to break out of this place." The communicator went dead. Cassady closed it.

"Can he do that?" Blannon asked.

Cassady nodded. "If he can figure out how to activate the gun. Problem is, if he uses it to blast the hangar door, the hull will probably rupture."

Blannon stared at him. "He'd be just as dead as the rest of us."

"Maybe not, inside the *Wasp*. Besides, I don't think we can count on Troy to make rational decisions."

"Let him take the *Wasp*, then," Erek said. That seemed the obvious thing to do. "The Guard will be here in less than an hour. They can catch up with him."

"I'd rather let him blow this ship up with everyone aboard than turn him loose with those interstream missiles," Cassady said. "God knows, I've made enough mistakes already without making another one of that magnitude. If he got loose with them . . ."

There was a long silence. Gillie finally broke it.

"Maybe we can let him go, but make sure he doesn't get far."

They all turned to look at him.

"I know quite a bit about these warships," he said. "Me and Uncle Aaron used to build models out of kiki wood. Uncle Aaron said a Guard warship was a miracle of technology."

Cassady smiled grimly. "He was right."

"What do you have in mind?" Erek asked.

Gillie hunkered down beside them. The look of skepticism on Cassady's face gradually gave way to intense interest as he listened to Gillie's plan.

"My lord!" he exclaimed when Gillie finished. "That might work." His eyes narrowed on Gillie. "You've got Troy figured out all right. Where did you get an idea like that?"

Gillie grinned self-consciously. "Uncle Aaron and me used to play wargames." The grin widened. "I beat him once with this same idea."

"It's worth a try," Cassady said. "But first—"

"We're forgetting something," Erek said. "You'll be in there with Troy."

Cassady waved a hand. "That's no problem. The *Wasp* has two sections. The crew compartment is separate from the cockpit module. It's designed that way for safety reasons—if one part of the ship's hull is damaged, the crew can survive in the other part. When the time comes—"

Whatever he was going to say was cut off by the buzzing of his communicator. This time it was Lieutenant Hollins.

"I'm in the flight deck, sir. We've got the last of the brigs locked up in holding cells on the fifth level, port side."

"Good work, Lieutenant. Any casualties?"

"Thamison and DiMemmo, sir." Hollins's voice sounded steady, but Erek heard the strain just below the surface. Hollins was holding himself under tight control. "Do you want us to come up there?"

Cassady looked out at the *Wasp* for a long moment. Then his eyes went to Gillie.

"No, Lieutenant Hollins," he said at last. "Troy has taken control of the *Wasp*. He's threatening to blast through the hangar if we don't get it opened quickly. If he does that, the entire starboard cylinder may be in jeopardy. I want you to get the stasis techs off the ship on a code green. Use the shuttles from hangar two."

"Yes, sir." There was a brief pause. "That was code green, sir?"

"That's what I said. We can't take any chances, the situation being what it is."

"Right away, sir."

Cassady closed the communicator and clipped it to his belt.

"I think we can make it around that way," Erek said, pointing up along the curving floor to a shuttlecraft anchored ten meters away. "If we keep low, Troy won't be able to see us. From there, we can stay out of sight of the ship's external eyes." He looked at Gillie. "Ready?"

Leo Blannon had a confused look on his face. "You're going to try to get in there?"

"Nobody else can do it," Erek told him.

"What about them?" Blannon nodded toward the guardsmen inside the elevator on the other side of the hangar.

"They'd never make it. Not from there. Troy would cut them to pieces."

"Yeah, but—"

"Besides, there wouldn't be any way to get the plan across to them." He saw Blannon's eyes go to the communicator on Cassady's belt. "Troy would hear us if we used that."

Blannon turned to Cassady. "What about your lieutenant and the men with him?"

"It'll take them at least twenty minutes to get back

down here. The Guard will be here by then. Troy will never wait that long."

"We're wasting time," Erek said. They didn't have any choice. He wanted to get it done. He looked at Gillie. "Ready?"

Gillie nodded.

Keeping out of range of the *Wasp*'s exterior eyes, they slipped from behind the pylon and moved down along the flange of the landing strip to the anchored shuttle. From there they moved in a crouching run past the tail cone to the *Wasp*'s starboard side. Gillie knew where to find the opening to the service tubeway just below the curved housing of the starboard stasis engine. The doors split vertically and opened at the touch of the control panel beside them.

Erek hoisted himself up and over the sill. It was dark inside and even more cramped than he had expected. Gillie closed the door behind him and they began working their way forward on their bellies. The dim light and the hard graymetal floor with bare rivets around each plate made the going tough—especially on the knees. According to Gillie, they would have to go through the crew's quarters, then take another tubeway out through the base of the starboard wing to reach the service port for the powergun.

Suddenly Erek heard a voice. He froze until he realized it came from the communicator strapped to his belt. He had kept it open so he could keep track of what was happening. For Gillie's plan to work, timing was critical.

"We've got them all aboard, sir." That was Hollins. "Shuttles three, six, and eight. They'll depart from the inner docking hub when you give the order."

Then Cassady: "Begin the launch process now, Lieutenant." After a brief pause: "And good luck."

"Good luck to you, too, sir." The channel went dead.

Erek and Gillie emerged from the service tubeway

into the aft crew's quarters. Gillie sealed the door and they stepped along the narrow corridor to the forward section of the main cabin. The cockpit lay ahead, just behind the ship's nose cone. Two monitors on the bulkhead in the mid-fuselage were lighted—probably activated when Troy switched on the main cabin power. One of them showed a section of the hangar and the other a view of the cockpit.

Erek paused to study that one. The angle of sight was from slightly above and behind the seats, with a fish-eye view that picked up the entire cockpit. Victor Troy sat rigidly in the command chair, staring at the vidscreens above him. His hands rested on the console. As Erek watched, Xavier Cassady swung in through the hatch and settled into the pilot's chair beside Troy.

"Come on." Erek knew they didn't have much time left.

They moved past the monitors to another airlock door and found another tubeway extending beyond that. They worked their way along it until they found the service port at the inside base of the wing structure.

"How long will it take?" Erek asked.

"Couple minutes," Gillie answered. He lay his tool kit on the deck, opened it, and selected a wrench. A moment later he was working on the bolts of the facing plate.

Erek looked at his wristwatch. He hoped Gillie was right.

Chapter 20

CASSADY reached to the back of the console and toggled a banked row of switches.

"What's that for?" Troy demanded.

"Serialization checks," Cassady answered. "Stasis computer, drive system, cabin support—it all has to run through the cycle before the engines will fire."

"We're using too much time. Can't you override it?"

Cassady shook his head. "It's built in. If I tried that, the whole ship would shut down." He reached above him and thumbed another switch, watched the readout screen as numbers built across it. Troy fidgeted in the seat beside him for a few minutes. Then:

"Why is everything taking so long?"

Cassady turned toward him. "Calm down, Victor. You can't just hop in a ship like this, turn on the engines, and take off. You have to follow certain launch procedures." Cassady gambled on his hunch that Troy wasn't familiar enough with these warships to see through the bare-faced lie. One of the greatest advantages of ships like the *Wasp* was that they could be made ready for flight on a moment's notice.

"The Guard will get here in less than thirty minutes," Troy said. "You have fifteen minutes to get this ship out of here and set on a random skip. If you don't do it by then, I'll do it my own way."

Cassady didn't have to look to know that Troy's hand rested on the firing bar for the nose powergun. The safety shield had been unlocked and already lay open when Cassady came into the cockpit. The gun was armed and targeted on the hangar door. He knew he couldn't stall much longer.

As Cassady turned back to the console, a telltale began winking on the stasis control board. The airlock door behind the cockpit module had been opened. He glanced sideways at Troy, but Troy's eyes were on the vidscreen. Cassady leaned forward casually and swung his leg up as if to find a more comfortable position, positioning his foot in front of the light to block it from Troy's view.

The winking light meant that Erek Speros and the boy had gotten past the crew's quarters and into the tubeway. It should take them only a few minutes to cut the cables and get back out through the airlock to the cabin module.

He cast another sideways glance at Troy and wondered if he could wait that long.

The bolts wouldn't come free.

"They've been stressed," Gillie said with a disgusted tone. "No reason for that. Whoever serviced this probably used a power wrench. He didn't know what he was doing."

Erek laid the wrench down and mopped his brow with the back of his arm. He had hoped that his added weight would be enough, but it wasn't. "What do we do now?"

Gillie was already looking around. "Only other way

to get to the powergun circuits would be through the cockpit. We can't go—'' Then he stopped, his eyes following the tube that ran down along the main wing support strut. Then he shook his head. "Naw, that's no good.''

"What were you thinking?''

"Well, we could . . . '' Gillie hesitated again. "Powerguns put out a lot of heat.'' He tilted his head toward the tube. "That's the exhaust outlet. If we could plug it, the gun would overheat. We might be able to get the same effect we were after in the first place.''

"How could we get in there to plug it?''

Gillie pointed to an access plate a few meters down on the side of the tube. "There's probably a filter in there. If we had something to plug it with . . . '' He let the words trail off, his mind already working on the problem.

Erek eyed the port dubiously. "What if we're in there when Troy fires the gun?''

"We're fried,'' the boy answered frankly. "But we can't do it, anyway. There's nothing around here that would stand up under the heat.''

Erek's mind had already been working on that. "Maybe there is.'' He moved down to the access plate and began removing bolts. "Remember those storage lockers we passed?''

"Yeah?''

"We'll find some emergency lifesuits in there. A few of those should do the trick.'' The facing plate came free. Erek set it aside and got to his feet. "Let's get them.''

"Time's up,'' Troy said. His hand moved closer to the powergun control. "I'm blowing us out of here.''

"You can't—''

"*Yes, I can!*'' Troy shouted. "And I'll do it right now!''

"Think about it,'' Cassady said. *Keep him calm for*

just a few more minutes. "If you do that, you'll prob-ably destroy this ship at the same time. What'll you gain by that?"

"You're trying to hold me until your Guard friends can get here." Troy's voice had dropped to a low, wavering tone. He swiveled the seat around so his eyes were fixed on Cassady. "It won't work. We're going." His hand lowered to the control bar.

"Wait!" Cassady snapped. Troy blinked, hesitating. Cassady waved his hand vaguely at the winking lights on the console. "Systems checks are all completed. We can launch now." He knew he didn't have any choice. Troy would follow through with his threat—there was no doubt of that.

He reached forward and keyed in the commands to the docking computer. The seat clamps folded in auto-matically around him. From the corner of his eye, he saw clamps fold around Troy at the same time. Troy struggled against them.

"What's this—"

"Safety harness," Cassady answered smoothly. "Stasis drive won't engage without them." Another partial truth. The system had an easy override, but Troy obviously didn't know about it. Cassady studied the console in front of him. The amber light still glowed, meaning that Speros and the boy were still back there.

Cassady knew that his chance for survival was gone. But Speros and the boy had one slim chance. Cassady hoped the boy knew as much about Guard warships as he claimed.

"That should do it," Gillie said, moving back from the filter to look at their handiwork, his face streaming sweat. The tube was solidly blocked with dozens of lifesuits that Erek and Gillie had carried in and jammed against the filter. There was no way to pack them as tightly as Gillie had hoped, but he had explained to Erek that the powergun exhaust should press them against the filter, blocking the tube more solidly.

Erek followed Gillie back out to the tubeway. They replaced the facing plate and squirmed backwards to the main cabin. Erek glanced up at the cockpit monitor. Troy and Cassady still sat in the control seats. Gillie was beside him.

"We did it," he said. "Now all we have to do is get back out—"

Then Erek felt movement and had to grab for a safety rail before he regained his balance. It took him a moment to realize that the landing strip under the craft had begun to slow. Erek and Gillie grasped the safety rail as the tug of gravity diminished.

"He's getting ready to launch!" Gillie said incredulously. "Doesn't he knew we're still in here?"

Erek stared up at the monitor. Cassady's hands worked at the control panel.

"He knows," Erek said. "But he doesn't have any choice."

"We have to get out of here. We—"

The craft lifted off the strip and Erek felt the sensation of movement as the stasis jets fired briefly. From outside he heard the rumble of the hangar door.

"Come on!" Gillie yelled.

"What—"

The boy was already pulling himself hand over hand along the rail. "The cabin's a separate module from the cockpit," he yelled. "If Cassady knows we're in here, he must be getting ready to cut us loose!"

Mystified, Erek followed the boy to the main cabin. He could already hear the sounds of decompression in the transit tube and the mechanical sounds as the airlock door began to close. Then Gillie was past the airlock, already pulling the door closed. Erek twisted around to help him, fumbling in the zero gravity. The door sealed with a sucking sound. A moment later he felt several jarring thumps.

"He's released the cabin," Gillie said, still panting. "That was close."

Erek had to agree. On the monitor, he could see the blackness of space, and the cone shape of the cockpit module drifting away from them.

Watching the system lights, Cassady keyed commands into the console to set up the drive system. He was certain Troy wasn't even aware he'd released the cabin from the rest of the ship—and he'd made sure the crucial vidscreen in the bank above the console was blanked before he gave the command . . .

"Ah, what's this?" Troy said.

Cassady looked up as the first of the stub-nosed shuttles came into view, rounding the curve of *Copernicus*'s massive port-side cylinder. Troy touched a control on the weapons board. The big powergun swiveled toward the shuttle.

"What are you doing?" Cassady asked.

Troy smiled grimly. "Call it venting frustration."

Cassady licked his lips. "Those shuttles aren't even armed."

Troy held the sizzler steady on Cassady, but his eyes remained on the vidscreen. His hand went to the powergun control.

"Wait—" Cassady began.

The flare of the powergun lighted the vidscreen as it lanced into the first shuttle. The hull glowed, then erupted in a bright flash.

"Why?" Cassady asked. "You're free now. Why would you want to do something like that?"

Troy didn't answer. The other two shuttles had taken evasive action, but too late. On the weapons scope, the powergun tracked the second one. The firing bar clicked again and the shuttle flashed out of existence.

Cassady saw a pair of lights on the console go amber, then red. He swung around to block them from Troy's view, although he doubted that Troy would have noticed anyway. His attention was on the destruction he was causing.

Troy lined the powergun up on the third shuttle and pressed the firing bar. As the shuttle flashed, a skin-creeping alarm filled the cockpit. Troy whirled around.

"What's that?"

Cassady smiled grimly.

"*Answer me!*" Troy screamed.

"The powergun is overheating," Cassady said calmly.

Troy's eyes widened.

"We knew you wouldn't be able to resist the bait of the shuttles," Cassady went on. "That's why I ordered them out."

Troy jerked his head forward to break off power to the big gun.

"The shuttles were empty," Cassady went on. "Operated by remote. Code green—that's what I gave Lieutenant Hollins. In our unit, that means a decoy. All the stasis techs are still aboard *Copernicus*." His eyes went to Troy's frantically moving hands on the power-gun controls. "Too late for that. The stasis engines are already out of temperature balance. They'll explode and there's no way to stop them. We have maybe twenty seconds."

Troy threw down the sizzler and began pawing at the seat clamps. A whimpering sound came from deep in his throat.

"You'll never make it," Cassady said. Through the seat he felt a deep vibrating power building up. "Any second . . ."

On the monitor, the blue-white flash lasted only an instant.

The cabin module had fired automatically to move it away from the *Wasp*'s cockpit module. The shock wave gave them a brief shake and moved on. Gillie blinked and looked away from the module.

"I wish—" he began, but the words choked off.

Erek looked at his wristwatch. The Guard would be arriving in less than five minutes. He settled down to wait with his back to the wall.

"What'll happen now?" Gillie asked. "Will Lieutenant Hollins and those other guardsmen be in trouble?"

"Probably," Erek said. "They're finished with the Guard, that's for sure." He shifted to a more comfortable position. "But they might consider that what they've done was worth it."

Gillie looked up. "What do you mean?"

"They got attention. I think that's what Cassady wanted all along." Erek had gotten the story from Kurt Hollins at the ECC, then more pieces from Leo Blannon in the hangar. "Cassady may have gone about this the wrong way, but he was right about one thing—the Fringe needs better protection."

"You think this will make a difference?"

Erek's eyes went back to the monitor: *Copernicus* against the brilliant backdrop of Omega Centauri.

"Leo Blannon's one of the best investigative reporters around," he said to Gillie. "People pay attention to what he says. Leo will make sure that what happened out here makes a difference."